DATE DUE

I'm

not

dying

with

you

tonight

I'M NOT

DYING

WITH

YOU

TONIGHT

KIMBERLY JONES
GILLY SEGAL

sourcebooks
fire

Published by Sourcebooks Fire, an imprint of Sourcebooks
P.O. Box 4410, Naperville, Illinois 60567-4410
(630) 961-3900
sourcebooks.com

Library of Congress Cataloging-in-Publication Data

Names: Jones, Kimberly (Kimberly Latrice), author | Segal, Gilly, author.
Title: I'm not dying with you tonight / Kimberly Jones, Gilly Segal.
Other titles: I am not dying with you tonight
Description: Naperville, IL : Sourcebooks Fire, [2019] | Summary: Told from two viewpoints, Atlanta high school seniors Lena and Campbell, one black, one white, must rely on each other to survive after a football rivalry escalates into a riot.
Identifiers: LCCN 2019008892 | (hardcover : alk. paper)
Subjects: | CYAC: Race relations--Fiction. | Riots--Fiction. | African Americans--Fiction. | Atlanta (Ga.)--Fiction.
Classification: LCC PZ7.1.S3386 Im 2019 | DDC [Fic]--dc23
LC record available at https://lccn.loc.gov/2019008892

Printed and bound in the United States of America.
WOZ 10 9 8 7 6 5 4 3 2 1

For Drake.

—K. J.

For Kate, who knows why.

—G. S.

"We didn't understand that the riots had begun…"

—*Bart Bartholomew,* New York Times *photographer and only professional journalist in South Central Los Angeles when rioting broke out following the Rodney King verdict*

I'm

not

~~dying~~

with

~~you~~

tonight

PART I
MASS DISTURBANCE

1

LENA

McPherson High School

"Waiting for Black is on your agenda, not mine," LaShunda barks as we leave the building.

I ain't think she was gonna wait, no way, that ain't what I was anticipating. *I* know she's got responsibilities at home, but *she* knows I hate sitting out here by myself. If you ask me, this is really about her hating on Black. As usual.

"It don't cost you nothin' to walk away," I snap back.

LaShunda cackles. "Can your grandfather stop speaking through your body?"

"I don't know what you talkin' about." I flip my hair over my shoulder, but she got me laughing like she always does. "Pops got all the best sayings."

She shakes her head and then looks down at my feet. "Anyway, I see you got them."

A big smile takes over my face. LaShunda never misses

anything I do. She knows me, like, really knows me, and she knew that statement would perk up both our moods.

"They cute, right?"

"Lady, you know they better than cute—they are fire, best friend. If I thought I could cram my size tens into them, I'd be trying to borrow them ASAP," LaShunda says.

"I saw some size tens in a different style as cute as these. Let me turn a few more checks, and I'm going to hook you up."

"Go, best friend. That's my best friend," she sings, and we both laugh. Her granny, Miss Ann, house is really her house. Miss Ann works two jobs and drives for Uber. LaShunda does all the laundry, cooking, and watching of her three bad, little cousins. Even though she works real hard, she's not able to have an after-school job or anything. That's why I love splurging on a pair of fly shoes for her when I can. I like being that person in her life who gives her the little extras. "So are we going to this game-slash-fund-raiser-slash-turnup-slash-piped-up lituation?"

"Yes, ma'am, you know if we don't see the Dolls dance at halftime, they will kill us."

"You ain't never lied." LaShunda winks. "NaNa, let me get out of here before Gram kills me."

"Okay, but don't flake tonight."

Anyway, it's okay she has to go. Some days you just want to be alone with your man, and for me, this is one of

4

those days. I've been missing him. He's been grinding so hard lately that we never get to see each other. He always smells good enough to eat. He puts aftershave right on his neck too, because he knows I like to rest my head on his shoulder and just breathe him in. Ooh, that man does something to me. He makes my head spin. I'm so caught up thinking about his fine self that I don't notice LaShunda walking away until she yells back at me.

"Love you later."

"Love you later," I shout. She hates goodbye. That's the last thing her mom said to her before she passed away from a heroin overdose. She's never said the word *goodbye* to anyone since.

I think about texting Black but that will only aggravate him. I know he's coming, and he always says what's understood doesn't need to be said. Not a minute later, he pulls up, bumping the new Kelechi album loud as he can. He has such amazing taste in music. He can't stand trap music and only listens to real emcees who don't do all that cursing and hating on women.

"Did somebody request an Uber?" He smiles, leaning toward the passenger window.

"I did. I hit the button for cute, so I wasn't expecting fine. Is it the same fee?"

"Uber Black is usually a little more, but I lower the rate when the rider is fine too."

We both laugh, and I get in. I lean over to hug him, and he smells as good as I expected. I almost don't want to let go. I lift my face for him to kiss me and melt into him. His soft lips press against mine, and it feels like sun rays warming my skin.

I gently pull away. "I need to go home and get myself together to be cute at the football game tonight."

"The game?" He starts the car and pulls out. "Since when is that something you do?"

"My girls doing the halftime, and I'm a good friend, jerk." I push his shoulder playfully. "But you know, I don't plan on staying longer than their show. So I'll have some free time left before curfew."

"Okay, well, Imma see how I'm movin' tonight, and you know, I'll let you know what I'm doing."

"So, that's a no?" I say, feeling my mouth twist up.

"I didn't say no."

"You didn't have to," I say. "I guess we'll see, won't we?" We pull up a few doors from my house, and I let him kiss me goodbye. "Bye, Black."

"Later, beautiful."

I roll my eyes as I get out of the car. I walk in my house and head to the kitchen for a snack.

"What you doing?" Pops asks, not looking up from the sink as he washes the plates. I have no idea why my grandfather won't use the dishwasher. I refuse to hand-wash dishes, my nails too delicious to be ruined by Palmolive.

"Just making a snack before I get ready for the game."
I sigh. Black usually leaves me in the most amazing mood, except for when he plays like he Hansel, leaving me crumbs.

"What's got you down in the mouth?"

"Pops, you ain't even looked at me."

"Don't need to. I can hear it. I reckon it's 'cuz of that little knucklehead you just got out the car with."

"Pops, I didn't—"

He interrupts, "Go to lying and the only game you gon' see tonight is *Wheel of Fortune* on the Game Show Network. If you had a nice boy, there would never be a need to lie."

No, if you gave him a chance, I'd have no need to lie. If I said that out loud, he'd pop me in the mouth. "Am I excused?"

"Go on, little liar on the prairie."

I don't care what Pops says as long as he don't say I can't go to the game. Imma try to hook up with Black later. I think tonight can end better than we just left it in the car.

2

CAMPBELL

McPherson High School
Football Field

My dad's truck rumbles into the school parking lot at the same time as the bus carrying the opposing team. We squeeze into a space at the very end of a row.

"It's good you're doing this, Campbell," Dad says, as the bus empties and a long line of beefy football guys in tracksuits lumber out.

Is it? I stay in my seat, remain buckled. I wonder why he thinks it matters if I work the concession stand for one game at this school. I'll only be here a year—my senior year. Where does he think this one night is going to lead?

While the players head through a gate in the chain-link fence toward the locker rooms, another bus pulls up and hems us in. This one lets out a load of cheerleaders, a dance team, and some boosters. The Panthers and their entourage fill the parking lot. According to what our principal said on the morning announcements, Jonesville is McPherson's biggest rival, ranked one beneath us in the standings. Or something. I guess they would bus in a big crowd for such an important game.

The only people around seem to be Jonesville fans. You'd think McPherson fans would've shown up by now to cheer on the home team at the most important game of the season. Then again, the principal made a big deal about expecting extra security and demanding we all be on our best behavior tonight, so I'm guessing the rivalry gets intense. Maybe it's better if the Jonesville superfans are settled on the visitor side of the stadium before the home crowd shows.

I look around for people I might know, then realize that's ridiculous. I don't know anybody here.

The human throng before us parts, allowing a tall woman with waist-length braids to make her way through. She struggles to push a dolly in front of her with one hand and drag a battered, red wagon behind her with the other. Both are heaped with cardboard boxes.

"That's Ms. Marino," I say. She coaches the dance team, teaches my English class, and invited me to work the concession stand tonight. I unbuckle my seat belt and hop out of the car to help her. To my surprise, my dad jumps out too.

"Campbell!" she exclaims. "So glad you decided to come."

I can't think why I did. Ms. Marino explained that this year, the proceeds from concession stand sales will be used to fund renovations to upgrade the rest of the athletic facilities so they'll be as nice as the fancy new football field. The only catch is, the teams have to man the stand. Of course, as the athletes are too busy during games to work the booth, they've been asking for volunteers. I didn't raise my hand when Ms. Marino asked, believe me. No one did, even though she practically begged for help every single day this week. The entire class dodged her. The awkward silences that followed her more and more desperate requests made me squirm. That's probably why, when she caught me as the bell rang this morning and asked if I'd ever run concessions before, the word *yes* came out faster than an excuse.

My dad takes the dolly, I hoist a couple of boxes off the top of the wagon, and we follow her toward the main gate. She leads us past two dance team members raising a glittery SUPPORT FIELD RENOVATIONS banner up to the top of the fence.

"Good job, girls," she calls. "Finish hanging that, and I'll meet you in the locker room in ten minutes for warm-ups."

The familiar ring of a coach giving orders makes me flinch. Words like those reverberated through my nights and weekends once. Back when I used to be on a team.

I look quickly away from the girls and their mascot-logo warm-up suits, and scurry after my dad and Ms. Marino.

The huge concrete stadium looms above us, casting a shadow over the concession stand, which is a relief. There's a good couple of hours of daylight left, and this wooden booth will be enough of a sauna without sitting in the middle of a sunbeam. The shade is the only thing to get excited about. Otherwise, the concession stand is a disaster—a rickety box built of plywood and two-by-fours, with big windows on one side covered by a rolling metal security grill, and below them, a lip of wood that juts out and is probably supposed to be the service counter. Ms. Marino dials the combination of a padlock hooked onto a hasp near the top of the door, slides it off, then yanks the door open, the knob wobbling loosely in her hands. With her, my dad, me, and the dolly, the booth is crowded to capacity. A third of the boxes and the wagon are still outside.

How is this going to work?

I don't point that out, though. I just help ferry the boxes.

My dad stays long enough to help cram all the supplies into the concession stand. "Okay," he says, when the last of the packages have been shoved into cabinets. "I'll see you after the game, Campbell. Pick you up right outside the gate."

"You know," Ms. Marino says. "The dance team always celebrates at Mr. Souvlaki's after home games. I think, after working the booth for us tonight, you've earned honorary team member status. You should come with us."

I'm stunned. "I don't really know any of the girls."

She smiles gently. "This is how you get to know them."

"Mr. Souvlaki's?" Dad's frown lines cut deep into his face as he considers this invite. "That Greek place up on Woodland Street?"

"Yes," Ms. Marino says. "Pizza's perfect, Cokes are cold, and they're both cheap! And I'll be there, as will both of our team moms. Plenty of adult supervision, if that's what you're worried about."

"Campbell, I was planning on heading up to the cabin right after the game. I'm not thrilled about getting up there that late," says Dad. He sets a hand on my shoulder, like his trip is breaking news to me. Like I'm disappointed and need comforting.

"You're going out of town?" Ms. Marino asks, deflating.

"Just him. But he's my ride home, so." I feel a strange mix of regret and relief churning around in my stomach. "Maybe another time."

"Oh," she says, her smile back and beaming. "That's no problem. I can drive you home after dinner."

What? No, no, no. As if being the new girl isn't pathetic enough. Now Ms. Marino is my ride?

Dad says slowly, "That could work. If I leave now, I'll reach the cabin before it gets too dark."

I protest, but in vain. My teacher and my father lock down my Friday night plans, he happily heads off to his fishing cabin, and before I even make sense of how it happened, I'm escorting Ms. Marino as she goes to get more supplies. We head toward her portable classroom, which is housed in a big square trailer on cinder blocks between the main building and the football field. The portables were probably meant to be temporary, housing overflow classes until the district could add on to the building, but as far as I can tell, they look like they've been there for about thirty years. Ms. Marino chatters on about wanting to have the best sales records tonight of any other team that's taken a turn running concessions, telling me the rules of running the booth. They're nothing new—take this seriously, give accurate cash back, blah blah—but everything else here is. Her words wash over me as I wipe the sweat from my forehead and let my mind wander to what might be happening back home in Haverford. Which I shouldn't think of as home anymore, since I probably won't ever live there again.

"This fund-raiser," Ms. Marino says. "It's partly about raising money to renovate the concession stand. It's such a disgrace compared to the new stadium. All kinds of donations welcome—construction supplies, for example."

Ah, there's the ulterior motive that isn't related to my popularity status. She knows my dad owns Carlson's Hardware down in the commercial district on Seventh

Avenue. She can't have ever been in the place, though, if she's hoping he's got anything extra to donate. I smile blankly back at her, pretending not to get the hint.

She doesn't seem to take it personally. She shrugs and hands me a small, metal lockbox, preloaded with quarters and singles, and the key to the room. "Here you go. Since your fellow salespeople haven't shown yet, you go ahead and take this down to the stand. You're in charge of it. I'll send them along soon. Meet me back here after the game so we can go to Mr. Souvlaki's! Wait inside, though. Don't stay out there with the cash box."

An hour and a half later, I'm still sweating my butt off inside the concession stand. It's not quite halftime yet in what has to be the longest game ever recorded. There have been so many penalties and stoppages in play I've lost count.

Ms. Marino came by a few minutes ago, took one look at the inside of this stand, and blew her top. "Y'all," she said, her voice snapping like a brittle twig. "You been having a food fight up in here? Get this place cleaned up. Now. I'll be back in the second half, and it better be as clean as the Board of Health."

"I'm gonna get supplies." Keisha swings her purse over her shoulder and heads for the concession stand door. "You stay here, New Girl, and start cleaning up."

"It's Campbell," I say. I told her that earlier, but she doesn't remember. Or maybe doesn't want to remember.

"Uh-huh, New Girl."

These are the first and only words Keisha has said to me all night.

That leaves me and Caleb in the booth, and he's no help. He only looks up from his phone to talk to a parade of friends, who, for some reason, keep stopping by the door, instead of the customer service window.

"Hey, dude," Caleb says, hopping down from the counter as another of his friends sticks his head in the door.

So here I am, the new girl, basically alone, cleaning up a catastrophic mess by myself.

People leaving me behind is quite the trend lately.

Somewhere overhead, people start cheering, and the band strikes up a song totally unlike the marching songs played at my old school. No John Philip Sousa here. Everything the McPherson band has played so far tonight could be on the radio. It's kind of awesome, and I wish I could be in the bleachers to watch, but I'm not supposed to leave the stand.

I glance from the pile of napkins scattered across the floor to the massive, old-fashioned soda fountain that's been jammed up and working erratically most of the night.

"What am I doing here?" I mutter.

None of the answers that pop into my head seem like good ones anymore. Yes, I worked concessions at Haverford, before my mom chased a job to Venezuela

16

and dumped me with my dad for my last year of school. Yes, the idea of working concessions and going out with friends afterward was the first thing that felt familiar since I moved to Atlanta. I imagine, for a second, an alternate universe Friday night in a similar booth with bright lights shining on the carefully tended turf of a football field. But those are the only similarities. All the rest of McPherson is so far away and so different, it might as well be another planet. In Haverford, October is already chilly. I'd be wearing my varsity track jacket, and I wouldn't be afraid to sneak out to watch the game. I'd be counting cash into a real cash register, instead of a metal lockbox, with people who were actually my friends. Almost half my track team, including my best friends, Lindsey and Megan, had been going directly from track practice to football games since freshman year. I'd be Instagramming pics of the architectural wonders we always built from candy bars when the game was boring.

I swing the door to the soda machine shut and think for a second about constructing a candy bar Golden Gate Bridge to post. There are enough Snickers bars to do it, but there's no one I could ask for help. Caleb's friend is gone, but Caleb has returned to sitting on the back counter, face glued to his phone. Anyway, I wouldn't want people in Haverford seeing this place in the background. Cellophane trails down the counter like enormous, shiny spiderwebs.

Trash litters the ground, including an entire stack of popcorn cups Caleb knocked over. They lay half crushed and blackened beneath our feet. A disgusting work of red-and-yellow abstract art, done in generic condiments, smears the customer counter. Ugh.

"Hey, Caleb. Do you think you could—"

Three knocks on the side of the concession stand.

"Hold that thought, dude," Caleb says. He jumps down from his perch and wrenches open the door, slapping hands with the guy on the other side.

I hold my breath for a second, trying to control the impulse to roll my eyes. And then, I bend down and start cleaning up. Not that I really want to. I don't want to be here at all anymore, but I can't leave. Anyway, my dad already left town for the weekend. There's no one waiting for me, even if I did take off.

Caleb hauls himself back onto the cabinet and pulls his phone into its usual position: in front of his face. His thumb scrolls and his eyes follow. Totally absorbed. I wish I had a snarky comment that would get him off his butt to help, but as usual, my mind's blank. I can only ever think of good retorts when it's way too late. Besides, I'm a little nervous to take a dig. I'm not sure how people here would react, and I am not about to risk starting trouble.

With a sigh, I start picking up dirty napkins and tossing them into a trash bag, keeping one eye on the kids outside the window. There's a few people hanging around, and I don't recognize a single one of them.

Except wait. There's Lena James. I know her—sort of. We have a class together, though she's never spoken to me. I recognize her friend too, the one Lena's always hanging out with. I can't remember her name. They're laughing as they wander over. Lena gives her friend a shoulder-shove, the girl shoves back, and then Lena swats at her with a Louis Vuitton purse. I look closer and see the leather is a little worn and the bottom is scuffed up, but I'm pretty sure that bag is not a fake. Wow. I wonder where she got a real LV.

Lena's forehead is beaded with sweat, and her makeup has started to cake. Surprising, since she usually catwalks the halls looking like she stepped out of a music video. Her long, wavy hair flows over her shoulders, and I wonder how she can stand the heat. Maybe she's compensating with her shorts, which are so short they've got to be a dress code violation.

I catch her friend eyeing me and realize I'm staring like a creeper. Whoops. I drop behind the counter, hiding from the girl's gaze.

3

LENA

McPherson High School
Football Field

The Dancing Dolls finish their routine, and everybody is going wild. My girl Aaliyah is the captain, and she was out front, crushing it. Next to me, LaShunda is Milly Rocking. I wave at Aaliyah from my seat as they're leaving the stadium. Then I grab LaShunda's elbow and pull her up.

"Come on, let's go before everybody else does."

"I still wanna see the band," she says. "They got one more song."

"You seen that tired-ass band before."

"You a hater," Shun says, but she follows me anyway.

Once we get done stepping over people and get to the bottom, a bass thumping hip-hop song makes just enough noise to be heard over the roar of the football stadium. The sound creeps through the leather of my favorite Louis purse—the one I searched for months to find—that special ringtone alerting me Black is calling.

He got his nickname from his family because his skin is darker than anyone else, but also because he was so dark and calm like a lake. The calm got lost when he got older, but he kept the name. If he was a girl, that rich sable tint would've gotten him made fun of, and for sure no one would have been checkin' for him to be a bae or boo. But being a dude, it made him a lady's man.

"Hey," I say, making it sound like I don't care at all that he called. I don't want him to think my world revolves around him. I mean, it does a little, but he don't need to know that.

"Hey," he says back, without the softness every girl wants to hear from her boyfriend—that tone in a guy's voice he uses only for you.

"Whatchu doin?" I ask, trying to draw him, like I usually can.

"Hangin' out."

"Who with?"

"You not still yellin' 'bout Tamika? She ain't even here." He definitely ain't sounding soft and sweet now.

That groupie who was all over him at the studio last weekend still causing trouble. He mad I said somethin'. But what was I supposed to do, let it go? Uh-uh. Anyway, that was days ago.

"I'm not."

The quiet is not good.

"What you doing later, shawty?" he asks, sounding like it's inconvenient to ask me.

"Tryna see you," I say with a hint of humor. I don't want to come off as thirsty. Everybody in our neighborhood recognizes Black, his box Chevy with the custom candy-purple paint, and his J's. I been wanting him, and now I got him and I plan to keep him, although it's work. Like keeping his age a secret at home. He's twenty. Pops don't know that. If he found out, I'd never leave the house again.

I wait to see what Black says, hoping he wants to see me too. I already miss the way he smells and the way he wraps his arms around me when he kisses me. I know I saw him earlier, but it was only a few minutes. I'm not trippin' though. He's been busy in the studio. His beats is fire. He's not gonna be a bum like the rest of these clowns who think they can rap. He says he'll do whatever to get rich. I believe him too.

I sigh a little when he teases back, "Aw, I feel special."

It's all right now. He ain't mad no more, and I can breathe easy. By the time we hang up, he's agreed to pick me up after the game. He's gonna get a new tattoo to celebrate almost finishing the new album, and I'm gonna hang with him and his boys while he gets inked. I hang up and can't stop smiling. LaShunda hits me on the shoulder and knocks me out of the trance I've been in since I heard his ringtone.

"Girrrrrl," LaShunda almost sings. "That must have been Black's annoying behind."

"Yup, so I don't need a ride home from you, friend."

We both laugh. I hope one day LaShunda finds a bae. I don't like candy, but I don't need it, because LaShunda is my sugar. She takes care of everybody from her baby cousins to me and anybody else who needs her. She thinks nothing of it. I see how amazing she is, but she doesn't.

I look over at her. "You comin' with me to meet him?"

LaShunda hesitates for a second. "Nah, I won't wanna hang around with them."

"Come on. A girl is only as cute as the cute chicks around her, and I need you to bring me up a few notches."

LaShunda shakes her head, like she don't think that's true at all. But of course, she jokes back. "Don't use me for my beauty. I have a brain."

"It ain't your brain I'm into," I say, and we both laugh, because most of the time, LaShunda is all about the brain. "Hey, remember that one time Black and his boys wanted to go to Stone Mountain, and we got on the kayaks, and the paddles got stuck, and you told 'em they had to row us back with their shoes?" I'm laughing so hard thinking about it. "Big Baby actually did it!"

"Yeah, okay. That was fun," LaShunda says. I can tell

she likes that memory as much as I do, and she wants to make me happy. She's smiling, but she's shaking her head. "I'm not comin' tonight, NaNa."

"Why? You do have fun with them. Come with me, and let's count how many times Wink flashes you that smile of his."

"He need to stop doin' that."

I grin, because I think Wink likes her a little bit and she kinda likes him too. "Don't front. You like that chocolate morsel."

"He a'ight."

"That smile is moonlight!"

"You mean sunshine. No girl wants that smile comin' at her at night," she says, nudging my shoulder and smiling for a second before her face gets serious again. "No. Uh-uh. Other than Wink, Black's friends are hella rude to me. You should say somethin' to your man when they talk to me like that."

Ugh. She right, and it ain't the first time she said it to me. I don't normally allow people to talk to me like that, but LaShunda's been my best friend since we was too small to know what best friends is. And she has a way of thinking that makes sense. She's always worth listening to. Black's friends might not treat her real kind, and Pops would comment on what that says about them if he knew. But I can't admit that to her.

25

I glance away and cross my arms. "Black just thinks you should have that kinda conversation in private, Shun. He don't want me frontin' on him with his boys."

"Well, as long as you ain't saying somethin', I ain't gonna come hang around his friends. You and me can find some other time to chill."

That hurts my feelings a little, but I would never say that out loud. Even to LaShunda. Anyway, I want to see my bae. That's what's keeping me going. Most people don't understand why I'm so pressed to spend time with Black. Everything about our relationship seems wrong on the outside, but it's our quiet moments alone that count.

"You should be glad I found someone that makes me feel beautiful," I say. "He tells me stories he don't talk about with anyone else. I know his dreams. Believe me when I tell you, ain't no one else get that out of him. He don't make a move without talking to me."

"Girl, Black do what he want," LaShunda says. "Anyway, that's what you offer him. What does he offer you?"

I roll my eyes. She thinks she has him figured out, but what she sees on the surface ain't what's really going on, and I don't gotta prove nothing to her.

"He's the one who noticed how good my style was. He's always telling me he's gonna put me to work being a stylist for him when he blows up." And he's right too. You give me fifty bucks and two hours at LaRue's consignment shop, and I'll have anyone looking red-carpet ready but unique. "When I told him about that cosmetology school me and Pops went to check out for me to maybe go to next year, he thought that was cool but said I could for sure do more. That's why I found the Art Institute. I've got a lot of style and a lot of opinion, and I need to put it to work."

"Well, he right about that."

I give her a little shove. "His boys call me the pretty bandit. I'm the first one to steal his heart."

"I think he did the stealing."

I grin. "I mean, I love him so much."

But LaShunda in serious mode. Unlike Black, I can never talk her out of being real when she in that mindset. "I don't know, Lena. Don't seem like he's there for you."

"He can be a little distant—"

"A little distant? Or are you a little clingy?"

"Excuse me, Lena James clings to no one."

"Me, Black, none of us can keep up with your demands."

I hate when she claps back at me like this. Especially saying that. She knew saying that would sting because a few times Black has stated it's hard for him to keep up with the schedule I request of him. I mean, I understand him. When he gets caught up at the studio, he in the creative zone. I get that. It's a little embarrassing, though, when LaShunda agrees with him.

"Just saying sometimes even I feel sorry for the boy. You're a lot," LaShunda says.

I glare at her. I don't like that response, and I don't like her making me sound like a thirst bot. "You are my friend. My friend, my side."

LaShunda lets out a long sigh. "I stand on the side of truth, and the truth is, you can be a gnat."

"Rude." I'm kinda surprised to see LaShunda being all Team Black. That part is not so bad, but I'm annoyed by all of it, so I need to get out of this conversation. The concession stand is right nearby. "I need a Coke."

"Whatever, NaNa." LaShunda flicks her hand and heads toward the stands.

I'm fine she walked off, though. Tomorrow we'll be laughing on the phone again.

The concession stand ain't exactly a 7-Eleven, but at least there's fountain Cokes. Except tonight, I damn near have to crawl over the nasty-ass counter to get the attention of the chick hanging out back there. She all crouched down for some reason.

"What you doin' down there?" I ask, staring at her.

When she finally looks up, she has the nerve to ask the dude, who clearly doesn't plan on working, to help her. I don't give a damn who gets my Coke, somebody just needs to get it.

"Coke," I say again.

Her ass is still moving slow!

"And don't take all night neither."

She finally gives me my drink, and I feel kinda bad for throwing my dollar at her and watching it fall in a bunch of ketchup. When I'm at work, people always rushing us to get their orders, and the owner, Dollie, is always sending me to calm people down. She don't like no kinda arguments, but she know I'm a boss and people love me. But even though I understand, this Coke is still nasty as hell.

"Ugh!" I slam the cup down on the counter. "What did you do to that?"

"Sorry," she says. "The machine isn't—here, let me get you another."

"No, gimme my dollar back. I don't want that nasty sh—"

That loud horn goes off, and I can't hear what ol' girl is talkin' about. It's a whole bunch of noise after that. People leaving the bleachers, cheering, all that. The band must be done.

4

CAMPBELL

McPherson High School
Football Field

"I'm sorry," I say, fumbling with Lena's condiment-streaked dollar. Her nostrils flare as she grabs the soggy bill with the tips of her manicured fingers. "I'm really sorry."

Kids descend from the stands in a stampede. The crowd is full of McPherson kids wearing school colors—black and gold—though not the official school gear sold by student council. They're in regular clothes, black T-shirts, bright yellow hats, and sneakers. That's familiar enough. In Haverford, people also wanted to be their own brand of school cool. The adults around all seem like they're connected with kids on the team, mostly moms decked out in PTO team booster gear and shirts with players' pictures screen-printed on the front and numbers on the back.

Outside the booth, a line of sweaty, cranky people forms. Keisha hasn't come back, not that I really expected her to. That leaves me and Caleb behind the counter, but he remains bent over his phone, ignoring me and the crowd. They've started yelling at us. At me.

Lena James is standing there, in front of the window, like she doesn't notice the crowd behind her. Like everybody can just wait their turn.

Nobody wants to wait tonight.

The line dissolves into a horde, as people press forward, calling orders, shouting over one another. I can't tell who's asking for what, or keep track of how much someone's order costs. No one will hand over their cash before I put the food in their hands, and I'm mixing it all up.

"Caleb, could you get the sodas?"

He doesn't respond.

I miss the system I had with Lindsey, Megan, and Rachael. We worked the concession shift together with as much precision as we ran the four-by-four. Handing off a hot dog and Coke combo isn't much different from handing off a baton. Lindsey took payment, Megan got hot dogs, I handled candy, Rachael was on drinks. We had bottles on ice in giant coolers, which was simpler than dealing with paper cups and a soda fountain. Everything was easier.

A girl calls me a nasty name after I tell her we're out of M&M's. I blame Caleb for that. He's been stealing and eating them all night. And definitely not putting any money in the cash box, despite the fat wad of dollar bills sticking out of his pocket.

It's got to be 110 degrees in here. I'm afraid someone is going to hit me. People in line seem so angry. Furious. I know I'm taking a long time, but what am I supposed to do? It's only me in here.

"Ew, gross," a girl shouts, when I try to hand her a hot dog. "You're sweating all over my food."

I blush, realizing I forgot one of those white paper sheaths before grabbing the dog. I try to apologize, but she flings the thing onto the counter, and shouts, "I'm not paying for that!"

I don't think we're going to be setting that sales record Ms. Marino was hoping for.

I sneak a quick glimpse at Lena, wondering what the queen bee thinks of the new girl. Huh. She's not sneering at me. In fact, she's holding her Coke cup in one hand and the dollar I returned to her in the other, and she looks mad, but she's looking away from me, staring down the girl shouting at me.

"Calm down," Lena snaps. "Whatchu want her to do? She might as well be back there all by herself. White boy ain't much help. You don't need that extra hot dog, anyhow; you can afford to miss a meal."

I blink. I can't believe she stood up for me. I can't

believe she said that either! I'd never have the guts to burn someone like that, but I *want* to. I offer Lena a small smile as thanks, but she rolls her eyes and turns her face down to the screen of her phone.

The more people crowd around, the worse the heat gets. Foreheads drip. Baseball caps get repurposed as fans, which don't do much beyond move warm air around. Voices grow loud, full of irritation and complaints. Mixing in with the black and gold of the McPherson crowd, there is a fair amount of Jonesville maroon and white. They wear official spirit gear—jerseys and T-shirts with huge snarling panther logos. The girls have pasted temporary tattoos of the mascot onto their cheeks.

I can't stop watching them. They remind me of my old school. My old friends. A lot. Maybe too much. A prickle begins high up in my nose, the warning sign that tears are gathering.

"Hey, you! What's wrong with you?"

A hand flies in front of my eyes, and I flinch. My cheeks get warm, and I hurriedly sniffle back the tear prickles. I've been standing there, staring. God, this is the wrong time to get all upset about missing home. Humiliated, I lumber back into action. Pass hot dog, take dollar bill. The line of people swells like a wave, pressing closer.

"You gonna move up?"

There's a guy, maybe three or four back in line, getting

restless. He's tall enough that I think he must be a senior, and he's got blond hair and a Jonesville soccer polo shirt. In front of him, a group of kids is goofing around. I can't tell which of them is in line, maybe all of them are, but they're all bunched up, pushing and shoving each other, paying no attention. They've kind of stalled the line.

"Come on," the Panthers fan yells, flinging up his hands. "Move already, boy!"

Oh, damn. I freeze. The guy in front of him is African American.

He stops and glances over his shoulder, looking for the source of the comment, and spots the Panthers fan. The noise in the immediate vicinity of the stand hushes a bit. The African American kid turns slowly. "What'd you say to me?"

The blond boy looks to his group of friends, all of whom have stopped messing around to focus on what's happening, and the Jonesville kid puffs up. "You heard me, monkey. I told you to move."

Oh. My. God. What a dick. That's so wrong—

A fist arcs through the air, thrown as fast as a blur, followed by the crack of knuckles into a jaw. I suck in air so hard and so fast, it hurts.

Not good. Not good. Not good.

A shout raises, and then more. The boys clash, chests bumping together, arms swinging. A boy stumbles, and his knees hit the ground. Fists batter downward, pummeling his head, his shoulders. His mouth opens in a cry I can't hear. The shouting has swelled again. Bodies tumble over and around the boy on his knees, and he's lost behind a forest of kicking legs.

I link my hands, crushing my fingers together. My breath comes too fast, making me pant like I've finished a sprint, though I haven't moved a step. I've never seen a fight up close. Every time a scuffle broke out in the halls at my old school, a teacher showed up in under two minutes to break it up.

No one steps in to stop this.

"Dude." Caleb has finally looked up from his phone.

A cup flies past, soda arcing through the air and splattering everyone.

"Aw, what the—"

"This is a new purse!"

And then things…detonate. One flying fist becomes twenty, fifty. Two bodies crashing into each other become dozens. Yells rocket into shouts.

Caleb comes to stand beside me. "This is intense."

Intense? *Intense?* This is way more than that. People push, shove, swing. Yell horrible insults I don't want to hear. Throw cups of soda, poster boards, pom-poms. A fan flag goes flying through the air and hits a woman in the side of the head. The crowd morphs into a huge, seething mass.

"We should do something," I say.

"Like what?"

"I don't know." How am I supposed to know what to do in a fight like this? Maybe there's someone I could signal. An adult who'd break up the fight. All the older faces I see are involved in the pushing and shoving. "Call for help, maybe?"

Caleb rolls his eyes. "You're an idiot."

He lifts his phone, and for a second I think, despite the name-calling, he's going to call 911. But he flips his phone horizontally and starts filming. Probably going live on Instagram, so he doesn't waste his front row seat to the show. What a jerk. Not a second later, the door behind us flies open. I whirl. Lena James, a dark stain seeping down the front of her cute outfit, bursts inside.

"You're not supposed to be back here," I blurt. Ms. Marino told us, clear as crystal. No friends in the booth.

Lena looks at me as if I've grown another head. My cheeks burn.

"Shut up, Becky," she says. "You don't see what's going on out there? Look what them fools did to my shirt!" She grabs a handful of napkins and swipes them across the stain. "There wasn't another one like it at LaRue's. I cannot show up to meet Black looking like this!"

I glance at Caleb. He's riveted by the fight, arcing his phone to film the chaos in panoramic glory. He couldn't care less that Lena's in here, that we're breaking the rules. Why do I?

Loud, older voices, sharp and authoritative, ring over the shouting.

"What's going on over here?"

"Break this up!"

To the right of the concession stand, two cops push their way through the melee. At the sight of the officers, my clenched muscles go loose with relief.

"Cops!" I say. "It's gonna be okay."

"Oh, now shit's about to get real," Lena says at the exact same time.

I turn my head, her eyes meet mine, and we stare at each other.

5

LENA

McPherson High School
Football Field

"Oh, clearly you don't know how this could go," I say as I roll my eyes.

Becky wrinkles her freckly nose. "And you do?"

This fool. I shake my head. "Don't you see those po po out there?"

This could go left, fast. And my damn shirt is ruined! I try to clean it up, but no luck. I'm so mad. Man, this sucks.

Some kids from the Panthers are holding down this big dude from my school, and he's trying to pull their hands off of him by peeling back their fingers. A couple rough girls are screaming at this chick from Jonesville, who doesn't seem to be that afraid of them. And there it is. A real brawl.

"Man," I say. "We already ain't feelin' these racist

Jonesville kids after that offensive-ass Halloween party incident, and now they have the nerve to come here, acting up?"

"Incident?" Becky asks.

White boy jumps in with the explanation. "When the football players dressed up in blackface?"

"Oh," she says, sounding real unsure. "Yeah, I heard about that."

Dude's still got his phone up filming, like he some kinda Ava DuVernay. "Who thinks that's okay anymore?"

"Anymore?" I say, staring. "Like it ever was okay?"

At least, he has the grace to blush a little. "You know what I mean."

"Unfortunately, I do," I say.

Outside the booth, I can't tell anymore what's happening, but sweat's flying, pieces of weave are hitting the ground, there's bloody knuckles, yelling, and cursing. Once it gets to this point, you better either get in the fight and go for what you know or get the hell on.

I'm about to get the hell on.

On my way into the concession stand, this one girl was swinging her purse so hard at the girl she was fighting, she hit me in the head. She didn't even look up. On a normal day, I probably would have swung on her, but I do not have time for that today. I ain't hurt, so I don't care enough to do nothin'. I don't want to be part of this.

And there's Becky's useless behind, standing around

looking like a garden gnome. This fool's first comment was that I'm not supposed to be here. I can't believe that's what she thinking about. I was tempted to bring the fight to this concession stand and give her a WorldStar beatdown for opening up her mouth to say some crap like that. But my mission is to lay low 'til everything dies down enough for me to run.

She's looking at the chaos. "What is going on?"

"Girl," I say. "They fightin'!"

I almost can't hear myself over the roar of the crowd. My ears hurt, it's so loud. I look over, and Becky's hands are halfway to her head, but then I think she realize how she would look, so she drops them to her sides.

The school resource officers step into the middle of the crowd. My eyes follow they dark uniforms, chests bulky with bulletproof vests, and I wait for their presence to bring more drama. I bet Becky is waiting for the people around them to settle down. That's because she ain't never been here when stuff pops off. She probably used to seeing how they treat white folks at concerts. This ain't that.

Officer Kersey slides in between two guys squaring off, a hand to each of their chests. He pushes them apart, hard, and sends the boys stumbling backward into other kids. Body-sized dominoes crashing into each other. All of a sudden, I peep this kid from my science class, Gabriel, trying to dump an extra-large Coke on a Jonesville kid's head. He hits Officer Kersey instead. The cop ducks and yells as ice and Coke go washing over his buzz cut. His partner, Officer Tate, grabs Gabriel by the back of the shirt and yanks him up until his heels leave the ground. The collar of his shirt pulls on his neck. Gabriel's flappin' around.

Oh, God. I hope this cop don't kill this dude right in front of me.

I breathe through my nose, and the humid air feels too thick. Too hot. Everything is too hot. My palms are sweating and my forehead is dripping and salt stings my eyes.

I look over at white girl. I bet she still thinks the officers will get this under control. That the people around will listen to them.

Stop.

Break this up.

Disperse.

They're shouting as loud they can.

Get on the ground.

Chill out.

Move along.

Becky can keep waiting. It's goin' down now. People are yelling at Officer Tate. He's tryin' to make room around him and Officer Kersey, backing up, using his elbows. Everyone's so wrapped in their feelings, nothing these cops do makes a difference.

"Does this happen a lot?" Becky asks, her voice all shaky.

Good lord. This girl.

"No," I say.

But white boy contradicts me. "Yeah, it does."

"When?"

"It's the third fight this season," he says, rolling his eyes at me.

"You mean somethin' as outlandish as this?" I wave my hand out at the crowd. "Nah. I would've heard about that."

"Not this bad, maybe," he admits. "Guess those other fights were before everyone in this town decided they hate each other."

"That ain't nothin' new," I say.

Becky looks between me and white boy, terrified. "What does that mean?"

She's shocked. Surprise, surprise. I decide I'm gonna ignore her.

The officers try to get the fighting under control, but it's not working. Folks are yelling, pushing, hollering about *pig this* and *pig that*. Like I said: Cops showing up did not make things better. Hope Becky sees that now. Before, people were just kinda acting a little annoyed. Hell, I thought for a second Becky's terrible customer service set off a brawl. But leave it to the police to really aggravate folks.

43

6

CAMPBELL

McPherson High School
Football Field

Lena, Caleb, and I stand behind the concession stand window, watching the seething crowd. Seems like hundreds of people are fighting. Maybe even thousands. Arms flying, feet kicking. The school resource officers can't control them. People are punching, pushing, shoving, and they're not afraid to hit the cops. I think they might be *trying* to. The officers are totally outnumbered. But they're also mad. I can tell they're scared, the way their voices sound. Loud and sharp. Repeating themselves. One of the officers elbows a girl in the chest. I didn't see what she was doing, other than running in his direction. Maybe he thought she was going to jump him. I can't imagine anyone being reckless enough to do that. She has to be a head shorter than him too, and half his size, especially with all his gear on.

He hits her, though, hard and violent, and she falls to the ground and cries out. So do I.

"This is awful. They shouldn't be doing this!"

"Never can trust the police," Lena says.

I meant *everybody*.

I feel exposed, standing here watching, and cross my arms, but my sweaty hands slide over my skin. I drop them quickly, wiping my palms on my jeans.

Lena's pissed. She stands beside me, buzzing with the fury of a hornet. But she's also breathing heavy, which makes me wonder if maybe she's as scared as I am. I have the worst impulse to grab her hand. Somehow, I don't think she'd like that very much, so instead, I tuck one shoulder behind hers. It's not much, but I feel less alone.

She doesn't seem to notice.

I want to go home.

"Should we get out of here?"

Lena holds a hand out, gesturing at the brawl in front of us. "Not yet. Do you see what's happening?"

Before I can answer—*boom*. A huge object crashes against the wall of the concession stand, hard enough to rattle the whole structure. I jump. Lena flinches. So do the cops. Both officers half crouch. One reaches for his hip and then—

A bang.

No. A pop.

Pop pop pop!

I freeze. The noise and chaos around me fade until all that's left are echoes of those pops for seconds that stretch longer than they should. Then I hear: "Oh, crap."

Behind me, both Lena and Caleb have dropped to their knees.

"Get down, fool!" Lena shouts. "They shootin'!"

That sound is unmistakable, though I've never heard it outside of a movie.

"They're shooting," I whisper. I'm only able to move my mouth.

Lena grabs my wrist and yanks me to the ground.

More popping. Then more screams. I don't even know who's shooting. The cops? Someone in the crowd? I peer up at the window, see heads bobbing around. A shaved head thuds against the wall of the concession stand.

There's an electronic screech and then the scratch and crackle of a walkie-talkie.

"Mass disturbance at McPherson High School! Shots fired, officer down!"

Oh, my God.

I'm trembling. My heart pounds. Lena's still gripping my wrist. She's not shaking, but her eyes are enormous. She's breathing fast again. Caleb mouths over and over and over: *Oh fuck oh fuck oh fuck.*

We huddle on the ground while chaos reigns outside.

Swearing. Screaming. Smashing. I turn to Caleb and Lena, but they aren't looking at me. His face is turned toward the window, mouth hanging open, eyes huge. He looks stunned. Lena stares at the wall in front of us, both hands over her mouth.

"This is out of control." The words don't come out right. They get caught in my throat, thick and dry like cotton balls. "This can't be happening."

7

LENA

McPherson High School
Football Field

"This, right here, is happening."

I'm stuck on the ground of this gross concession booth, which is wet and sticky and probably the most unsanitary place in the world, and the air still stinks from the gunshots.

The smell reminds me of the time they got to fighting at the Hype Awards. I was so excited to go. My auntie hooked us up because she works at the theater where they held the show. The smile on Black's face when I showed him the tickets was so big. It took me six visits to LaRue's, a month's worth of paychecks, and some extra cash from Pops to put my perfect look together. There was nothing hotter on that red carpet than my gold pantsuit. Black rented a Benz truck so we could flex on these people. He held my hand as we walked up. I was cheesing, the night was so perfect. Then, some fools got to fighting. The po po came, people started running and shouting. I couldn't move. Black pulled me, saying, "Come on, bae." We got up out of there quick, but before we could get outside— gunshots. I'll never forget that smell. If that fight hadn't happened, there'd have been a picture of me in that pant- suit on the entertainment blogs.

Anyway, sounds weird, but I'm kinda glad that hap- pened. Now, I know what to do in these types of situations. Lucky for Becky too, otherwise she might have gotten her head blown off.

White boy jumps up, and I cannot believe my eyes. Just when I gave this fool credit for not being a horror movie stereotype, he does the dummy, hopping up and looking all over the place. He knocks over a hot dog box trying to get to the cupboards. What the hell is he looking for?

He swings open a cupboard door and pulls out a red book bag. A bunch of small packs of weed go tumbling to the ground. Moving superhero fast, he swipes up the bag- gies, tosses them in the backpack, and takes a leap over us on the way to the door. His foot clips Becky's shoulder on the way down.

She shouts, "Hey!" But it's too late. The door to the stand flies open, and white boy jets.

I glance back at Becky. Her cheeks are red, her neck is dripping, and her freckles are more obvious. I touch my own cheek, and I'm warm too. I'm starting to think I was wrong. I'm starting to think it's time I left. I can usually count on LaShunda to save me. So I'm super regretting beefin' with her before. How long we been cooped up in here? I hope she ain't get caught up in this mess, but maybe if she still close by, she could come and get me.

I text her to check. *Girl, where u at?*

Home, where u at? W/ Black?

Not yet.

Not yet, NaNa, or never?

I don't have time for her nagging about Black right now.

It's hot up here so I wanna get out sooner.

She texts again right away. *U didn't get caught up in that fight I been hearin bout?*

Kinda. Come get me?

Can't, NaNa. Jaquavious got my car. Took it down to 7th.

What am I gonna do, Shun?

Lemme text Quay.

I check Becky—she's crouched on the ground near me, looking like she's about to cry. Tears filling up in her eyes and everything. "You better text somebody to get you," I say. "I'm working on a ride."

She looks at me like she don't understand what I'm saying. I shake my head. I tried.

What's Quay say?

Nothin yet. Want me to try my mom?

She's likely to be at the church function with Pops.

Nooooooooooooooo. Dear God please do not call your mom!!!!!!

Then u gotta wait on Quay, but u know how he is.

I put my phone away. I think I might have to call Black. I just need to get him on the phone, and he'll understand. This ain't about a hookup. This is serious business.

8

CAMPBELL

McPherson High School
Football Field

Caleb's gone. Vanished into the crowd with his cell phone full of videos and his backpack full of weed. I can't believe he had all that in there. I was tending the concession stand with a drug dealer and I didn't know!

It's pointless to worry about that, but easier to focus on it than anything else. Lena says I should text my ride. How am I supposed to do that? I don't have Ms. Marino's number. I can't exactly go out there looking for her, can I?

I don't want to think about that. I don't want to think about the gunshots or the fight or what's going on outside or what I'll do when we finally get out of here.

The flimsy walls rattle as two battling girls crash against the concession stand, stumbling through the open entry and falling in a heap.

"Oh, hell no," one of them screams. "Don't you be comin' at me!"

They wrestle until one girl scrambles up, her bright yellow tank top now smeared with dirt. The other girl cowers on the ground. Yellow Tank windmills her arms, battering and snatching until she comes away with a fistful of hair. The girl on the ground wails, covering the bald patch, and scootches backward out the doorway. As she runs off, shouting insults, Yellow Tank hoists the hunk of black hair like a trophy. But her victory strut doesn't last. A fully loaded hot dog flies toward her, hitting her smack in the face. She sputters, spitting out a mouthful of ketchup and mustard, and grabs a full cup of soda from the counter-top to return fire. Half the Coke spills when she winds up, splattering my sneakers.

"Hey!"

I clap my hand over my mouth, wishing I could grab the words and shove them back down my throat. I didn't mean to say anything, but I've caught her attention. She yells, "Shut up!" and pitches a water bottle at me. I duck and throw my arms over my head a second before it bounces off me.

Owwwww. That hurt. I back away, keeping my hands in front of my face.

"Girl, get the hell outta here," Lena says.

"Who you talkin' to?" She turns toward Lena.

Oh, God, oh, God. They're going to fight! In here! Should I try to stop them? Should I run?

As I try to figure out if I can escape before they attack each other, a pair of arms grabs the girl around the waist. She screams and flails, but the person drags her out the doorway. She disappears into the melee.

"Typical," Lena mutters.

Tears burn my eyes. I rub them hard, trying not to panic. I have to get out of here.

How do I get out of here?

"Black, I need you to come get me."

Lena's got a cell phone in one hand, and with the other, she points past me, jabbing a stiletto nail that winks with a press-on jewel. I gawp for a minute, and she snaps her fingers. Oh. The door still stands wide open. I crawl toward it. Lena wants me to shut the door, so that's what I'm going to do.

Outside, there's a pileup in progress. I stare, not comprehending what I'm seeing, not grasping the bodies flying at one another, diving into the fight.

And then there's someone coming at me. A huge African American guy, racing toward the doorway. Like he's going to bust in here. With us! I scream and shove at the door. The badly fitted wood scrapes along the dirt, catching on the debris that has been kicked inside during the fighting. I grunt, throw my shoulder against the wood.

The guy's here, he's right here, about to come in. There's a crack and I flinch, and then the door wrenches free and I slam it closed. Right in that guy's face. There's a boom, and the wall shudders as if he's pounding his fist. I use all my weight to shut him out.

Another slam jars my arms. My muscles clench.

I have to hold on. I grit my teeth and push against the rattling door.

The banging stops. The door stays closed and goes still after a second. I do not.

A wave of shakes crashes over me. I list into the door, letting it hold me up, and bring my hands in front of my face. Stare at them. They're filthy. Did I do that? Did I hold that guy off? Wow. My knees are wobbling, and I still can't hold myself up. As the last of the adrenaline burst fades, I buckle. Even the support of the door isn't enough to keep me upright anymore. I sink onto my butt, my head dropping heavily forward. My jeans are covered with dirt, gory, like I crawled through a mile of mud instead of a foot. The tears that have been gathering for the last fifteen minutes slip down my cheeks. I let them fall.

Outside, the fight rages. The power of it ripples over my skin, rattles around the empty space Caleb left behind. There's a million obvious reasons for him to run, but all my brain keeps wondering, over and over and over, is how he could have abandoned us.

With only me and Lena left, this shelter feels less like a fortress and more like a cage.

She barks into her phone, an older model generic one.

I try to hold myself still, winding my arms so tightly, they start to tingle like they're going to go numb. I catch sight of the security grill that goes over the windows. The pulley that lowers it is almost within my reach—if I stretched or maybe stood up, I could grab it. Should I do that? Would putting that down make us safer?

Lena's voice raises, and I glance over at her instead. She holds the phone right in front of her mouth, speaker so close, her lips touch the plastic. "What do you mean, you busy? Where are you?"

She sees me looking, and her face hardens. Her eyelashes flicker, then she drops her gaze to the ground and spins away. Hiding from me. Her shoulders hunch, like she can protect her secrets if she curls small enough. I shift on the ground and squeeze my eyes shut. I'm not trying to eavesdrop, but there's no privacy in this tiny little closet of a space. I can't stop hearing. She keeps talking, words coming faster, less carefully selected, and I don't like it. Lena barking orders, I can handle. Lena losing control? That I can't contemplate.

"No!" Her shout snaps my eyelids up. "You gonna die on me now, you raggedy piece of trash?"

She grips the phone in both hands, knuckles going

tight, then throws it in her purse. My already roller-coaster-wild stomach plunges.

"How am I supposed to get Black up here? Didn't even have a chance to tell him what was goin' on."

Okay. This girl cannot lose her cool. We can't both be completely freaking out. "Lena."

She spins back toward the window, pulling herself to her knees. "LaShunda, why'd you have to leave? Who else I know out there? I have got to get out of here and get to a phone."

Black dots float in front of my eyes, briefly obscuring Lena. Leave? Leave me here? Her too?

"I have a phone." The words are out before I think them through.

"Give it to me," Lena demands, instantly in my face.

"It's not here." I pat my pockets as if I'm looking for the phone, then spread my arms wide, showing her I'm empty-handed.

Her face crumples. Smoke practically starts pouring from her ears. "You think you funny? You think you any better off in here than me? They'll tear you apart."

"No! I didn't mean that. I left my phone in my back-pack. In my classroom. In the portables."

"Who the hell walks around without they phone?"

"I didn't think it was safe to bring my bag down here."

She huffs. "Great. You were so worried about someone stealing your phone, now we both stuck."

That's not fair! How was I supposed to guess an epic fight would break out and trap me in the concession stand with her?

"Look at these shenanigans," she says, her eyes on what we can see of the fight. "Okay, listen, here's what we gonna do. Far as I can tell, mostly they fightin' right outside, so if we can get around back of this stand, we oughta be able to get to the gym and around to the portables."

"What?" I look from her to the window. There's not much to see from this angle, but the shouting floats in nice and clear. The sirens too. "Leave? Like, this minute?"

"Didn't you tell me I could use your phone?"

"Yes, but—"

"And how am I supposed to use your phone if we don't get it from your classroom?"

"Well—"

"And how're we supposed to get to your classroom if we don't get out this concession stand?"

I shake my head. I want to leave, but I'm terrified to move. "It's not safe out there."

"You think you safe in here? How long before a bullet come through that window?"

Oh, my God. Everything is spinning, and my stomach rolls again. I close my eyes, but Lena grabs my face. Her touch feels like someone slammed the brakes on the world. But at least that stops the spinning in my head.

"You gonna get yourself together, Becky," she says, right in my face. So close I can smell the faintest traces of her flowery perfume. "We have to get out of here and get to your phone, and you can't be fallin' apart when we do."

She's crouching in front of me. Her knees are as dirty as mine. Mud-covered. Hers are bare, though. She'll wash up easier. My jeans are toast. I shake my head one last time. Lena's right. Someone out there—maybe more than one someone—is shooting.

I'm not safe here. Nobody is safe here.

My eyes lock on Lena's face. There's no more embarrassment. Her voice isn't shaking. She looks more like the put-together girl I always see walking around the halls, making everyone laugh.

I swallow hard and nod. "Campbell."

Lena squints at me.

"You called me Becky, but my name is Campbell."

"Like the soup?" Her tone is sharp, but her mouth curves up at one corner. It's nothing close to a smile. But it's there.

"Yeah," I say. "Like the soup."

"And people think black kids have stupid names." She shakes her head. "Okay, then, Campbell Soup. You ready to get ya ass outta here?"

"Yes," I croak, and then clear my throat and try again. "Yes."

"Good. When I open that door, we gonna run like hell. You follow me, okay?"

I nod. She grabs my hand, hauls me to my feet, and reaches for the door, all in one motion. The second she swings it open, a body falls through and crashes to the ground at our feet. And then another. There's a crush of people in the doorway, falling and shoving and piling up.

"We're trapped," I cry.

9

LENA

McPherson High School
Football Field

"Oh, hell no!"

I start climbing over people, pushing them out the way, stepping on them. I'm not excusing myself. I. Am. Out. Of. Here.

"Hey!" Campbell shrieks. "Let me out!"

I look back and see her trying to keep up as some bulky dude pushes a white guy off him. The white guy goes crashing into Campbell, grabbing onto her. I bet he's trying to stay on his feet, but the way he grab her, she ends up right between him and ol' Bulky. Bulky's wearing a red hat cocked to the left and a thick gold chain. His ass ain't in high school, I know that.

"Move, bitch."

White dude sees his chance and takes off, which is what

we need to do. But instead, I jump in front of Campbell. "Call her out her name again!"

He hulks up at me. "Whatchu gon' do?"

LaShunda always say my mouth gonna get me in trouble. Maybe this is that time.

"You ain't scare me," I say, ready to put him in his place.

He lifts one big paw and mushes me in my face, shoving me back. His skin is all sweaty and smells like funky feet. I stumble, because he pushed me hard, but I pop right back, raising my arm to let him have it.

Campbell grabs the back of my shirt. "No," she gasps in my ear. "No, no, no." I twist my head around to see her, and she's shaking her head. I get her message. We have to keep going.

She drags me back a couple steps. I point at Bulky. "You got lucky."

He lunges, like he's not gonna let it go. Campbell shrieks, and I jump back, chest heaving up and down. Is he actually gonna hit me? He can't hit me if he can't catch me. I'm not sure if I'm going to get away. Luckily, someone bumps him, and he spins. I got saved.

He gets back to fighting, and in a second, he's surrounded. Man, this is some *Hunger Games*–level stuff out here, so I start to Katniss my butt through the crowd. We're getting pushed around, bumped from every side, and we have to hold tight, so we don't lose each other. I gotta give it up to Becky—I mean, Campbell. She is thuggin' it out. Homegirl stays on my heels. In another minute, I see the gym and the covered walkway that leads back to the portable classrooms that ain't really portable since they been stuck in the same place since before my cousin Marcus went here. Most people are mobbing toward McPherson Road to get away from this fight, so it's only a few of people going where we are. I look around, and I see Tremaine holding his little sister Onicka's hand, and he's practically lifting her off the ground, he's running so fast toward the portables. When something ain't right, Tremaine definitely is one of the first people to remove himself from the situation, so if he's sneaking around this way, it's the way to go.

Campbell loosens her grip, but she don't let go. Thank goodness, because all of a sudden, the world goes dark.

I stop running, because what else can I do? If I move, I'm gonna trip.

"What's happening?" Campbell sounds as freaked out as me.

"I don't know," I say. I shuffle a few steps forward, bump into a post and grab on. We must've gotten to that walkway, but I can't see. I need a minute to think, but I'm afraid to stay still. I can't tell if something's coming at us in this dark.

Campbell's hand gets ripped from mine. She wails.

"What the hell, Campbell?"

"Someone bumped me. I'm okay. I think."

"Get up, get up!" I hear feet pounding around us.

And then, like a Beyoncé concert, cell phone lights start to go on. "Yes," I breathe.

Campbell gets to her feet, and we take off again. Sweat rolls down the line in the center of my back, and my hair is flying like a superhero cape. The noise of the fight begins to fade behind us, so I can hear both of our tired breaths and our feet slapping the pavement. My charm bracelets jingle on my wrist. Ah, these shoes makin' it hard to run. The straps are rubbing my toes into blisters, and my feet are starting to swell. These delicious gladiator sandals were not designed for this apocalypse. Ewww. I hate this night.

We get to the portables, and then I'm lost. "Which one?"

Campbell points. I can barely see without any lights, but her arm brushes past me. "There, number six."

When we reach the door, I yank on the handle. "Locked!"

After all that, we're locked out? I slam the door with my fist.

"Wait," Campbell says. "Wait. I have a key!"

"How'd you get a key?"

She bumps me out of the way and presses up to the door. There's fumbling, and the metal key scrapes around on the door as she tries to find the lock. "Ms. Marino gave it so me so I could meet her here and return the cash box— oh, no." The scraping stops.

"What's wrong? Let's go." I'm tempted to shake her, but I keep my hands to myself. "Get the key. Come on, why you trippin'?"

"I left the cash box. In the concession stand. When we ran."

"We don't got time to worry about that now!"

"I can't believe I did that!" she says. "The money's going to get stolen. Ms. Marino's going to be so furious at me."

I throw my hands up. "You don't think Ms. Marino will understand why we had to run? You think she cares more 'bout some candy money than you getting killed?"

Campbell pauses, then says, "Right. Duh. Okay."

The key scrapes the door again and then clinks into the lock. I'm almost on top of her as she opens the door.

"Yes!" I say, locking the door behind us. "Where's your phone?"

PART II

ALL
CALL

10

LENA

McPherson High School

"Hey, bae!" I can't believe Black answered on the first ring. I'm so glad he did.

"'Sup, shawty?" His voice sounds so steady and smooth, I relax for a second. "Who phone you on?"

"Campbell's. My phone dead."

"Campbell? What she look like? She got a fat ass?"

"Stop playin', Black. It's not safe down here! The police up here harassing people as usual, people running everywhere. Somebody got shot!"

There's a long pause. I wanna see how he's going to react. Is he at least gonna act like he's worried? He stays quiet, though. My shoulders droop.

"Black, I gotta get out of here before I mess somebody up."

Black laughs. "Girl, you ain't gon' do nothin' to nobody. What you gon' do, baby, put the chopper on them?"

"Whatever, whatever, what the hell ever," I snap. "I need you to come get me. I can't be here."

"You were about to buck on these fools a minute ago," he says, still laughing hard and loud.

"Shut up before I buck on you!"

"Slow down, killer. I don't want no problems."

"Guess what, Black? This is serious. Are you coming to get me or not?"

"Ummmm, for real-for real, I prolly can't. I'm over by the tattoo shop, and I don't really know what Peanut and them got goin' on. Soooooooo."

My blood is boiling. Before I can stop myself, my volume has gone way up. "So, you finna let me be out here with all this goin' on down at the school?"

"Damn, Lena," he says, and I do not like his tone. "You bein' real dramatic."

He did not just say that to me! "Oh, is that so? How 'bout I get Campbell's boyfriend and his friends to take me home?"

"Now you trippin'."

No, now *he's* trippin'. I recall all the times he's acted super jealous when someone else complimented me or made it clear they liked me. His nostrils flare, his lips tighten up, and he takes in this deep breath when he's getting irritated. One time I was at the studio with him, and the engineer kept looking me up and down. Finally, he said, "You look mad different today."

I came from a photo shoot that my hairdresser asked me to do. I'm always cute, but I can't lie, this particular day, they let me style the shoot and I went full-on glam squad. As a thank-you, they let me keep this one dress, and I was still wearing it when I met Black. I saw curves even I didn't know I had. Sure enough, within seconds of the dude staring, talking, complimenting, and smiling, Black's cute little nose flare turned into a full-on attitude.

Seems like when I need him to show me he cares in the way that means something to me, he can't. Why do I have to make him jealous for him to take me serious? Why did he answer Campbell's phone, a strange number, right away, but earlier I had to call him three times to get a response?

He's trippin', and I cannot wait.

"I'm not playing," I snap.

"Um, a'ight, uh, lemme see."

"What's all that, Black?"

"All what?"

"All that back and forth! Come get me."

If Black don't come through, I'll have to call Pops. Nobody else is left, and I don't remember any other numbers by heart. Pops would ask a lotta questions I do not want to answer. He'd find out I was lying about coming home with LaShunda. And since he don't drive at night no more because of the glaucoma, he'd have to call one of the church ladies to bring him over here. And that would piss us both off. I'd be on punishment for a month, and I'd miss the Atlanta Local Designz Pop-Up Shop. That would suck so bad.

Black has to come through.

I whip around and see Campbell. Hell, I forgot I was on her phone. I'm too mad to be embarrassed that she heard us arguing. I bet when she calls her boyfriend, he gon' be like, *okay, honey, I'm on my way.*

"Look, I told you I'm not down here by myself," Black says. "Might be some things jumpin' off later, and everybody rolled with me. I can't leave 'em stuck."

"You could try, though, Black! A real friend wouldn't want your girl out here like this."

I don't want to admit it, but that makes me kinda nervous where Black's friends are concerned. They been known to strand a girl. One time, they left LaShunda when there was no room in the car. That's the way they get sometimes. She called Marcus for a ride, and he called his momma, who called Pops. And then there was some real drama. I didn't like that they left her, but I wish she would've called anyone other than my cousin. That was the start of Pops setting rules about me seeing Black.

Black says, "A'ight, hold on."

I trust Black. Just not his boys.

I look down at my shoes. He must have put me on mute. While I'm waiting, I go back to the fact that he picked up the phone on the first ring. He don't never do that when I call from my number. It almost always goes to voice mail, then I text and he responds to my text. Now, he calls me and I answer. Funny how he answered a strange number right away.

What's taking so long? I want to hang up. If it was anybody else, I would.

The rumbling of voices resumes in my ear and loud music. "A'ight, shawty, guess what?"

"You're coming to get me," I say, as excited as a kindergartener headed to Chuck E. Cheese's.

"Nope. I'm in the middle of some business. But if you can get down here, Imma let Big Baby drive you home."

"Why can't he come get me, Black?"

"Look, Lena," he says, his voice all short. "You want the ride home or not?"

"Yeah, you know I do. Can't stand you."

He laughs. "I know what you can stand, though."

"No, you don't," I snap. "Wait for me, okay? Imma call you when I get close."

"How you gon' do that? Ain't yo phone dead?"

Dang, he's right.

I could walk down to Seventh. I turn around and look at Campbell.

"Don't worry about that. Stay by your phone."

11

CAMPBELL

McPherson High School

Lena ends her call and holds my phone out. "Thanks."

I nod, sliding it into my pocket. The room's dark, illuminated only by the faint reddish glow of the emergency exit sign, and the distance from here to the football field dampens the noise of the fight. In the relative silence, a wave hits Lena and me at the same moment. My legs go slack. Lena sighs and slumps into the chair behind Ms. Marino's desk. She clutches her purse to her middle, sagging tiredly around the shoulders.

If I sat down, I wouldn't be able to get up again. So I stand, awkwardly, fidgeting with the straps of my backpack.

We should be saying something. Goodbye, maybe. Since someone is waiting for her. She'll go soon, take off to meet that guy.

Leave me behind.

The room feels small and the air is heavy and it's too dark. Too quiet. Nothing good ever gets said into the silent darkness. Four months ago, my mother broke a hush like this to tell me she was moving to Venezuela for a new job. And leaving me behind.

She'd picked me up after track practice, the last parent to arrive, so the lot was empty and quiet and dark. I remember swiveling sideways in the front seat to stare at her when she put the car in park instead of backing out, and blurted the words.

"I'm moving to Caracas."

"What?"

"I can't say no. They're eliminating my position in the U.S. office. If I don't go, I'll be out of a job. What would I do? Now is a terrible time to be looking for a job. You understand that, don't you, Cam?"

I didn't understand, but I knew that tone of voice, the one she used when she said, *I can't afford to send you on the class trip to DC, Cam. It's $250; that's our gas and electric bills this month. You understand, right?* Or: *I can't make the district meet this weekend, Cam, I have to go to that golf tournament with my boss. I told you about that, right? But Dani's mom will take a video for me; I made her promise, so I can still see you race.* There were tears at the bottom of that tone. I'd say I understood, every time, no matter what, so long as she didn't cry.

"Okay," I'd said. "Venezuela. Is there, like, an international school I'll be going to? With all the diplomats' kids? Is there a track team?"

"Oh, no. That's not possible."

"My Spanish isn't good enough to go to school with native speakers. It'd kill my grades senior year—"

"Cam, I didn't mean no international school. I meant, you're not coming with me."

I felt like the car had slammed into a tree, though we were sitting still. "What?" I whispered.

"You're going to stay with your dad next year. Won't that be great? You've never had a chance to spend so much time with him. You'll have a much easier time transferring to another school in the U.S.—and more affordable too. And—and you'll still be able to run track. This is for the best. You understand, don't you?"

My mother's voice fades from my mind, and I try to shake off the hollowness that memory leaves inside me. It doesn't matter anymore. I'm here, a month into senior year at McPherson. But I still don't like the dark.

I feel around near the door frame for a light switch and then stop. The power is out. Anyway, I don't want to attract attention, don't want anyone trying to break in here, like they did at the concession stand. I step away from the wall, and it brings me closer to Lena, who's flicking at the screen of my phone with her thumb.

"You got a flashlight on this thing?"

"There's an app—" I begin, leaning over, but she finds it before I finish the sentence and ends up beaming me directly in the eyes.

"Ooh, sorry," she says, aiming the light down. I blink away the black dots that hover in my vision to find Lena's face a couple inches from mine. She's studying me with wide eyes surrounded by a fringe of superlong lashes. Fake ones? Probably. She applies them like a pro, if they are the glue-on kind. The only time I ever tried those, they ended up so crooked, it looked like my eyebrow had grown down over my eyelid.

I'm surprised she's still here, but I'm glad I'm not alone.

"Hey, um, thanks. For—" I wave my hand vaguely in the direction of the football field, the concession stand. "All of that."

She smiles. "That mess was too much for anybody to go alone, you know?"

I have no idea how to respond to that, so I kind of nod. Again. God, I hate myself for becoming a bobblehead.

Suddenly, Lena sits up straight. Her purse falls from her lap to the floor.

"Maybe somebody left a charger in here!" She begins yanking on the drawers of Ms. Marino's desk. Most are locked, but one slides open. I hover over her, watching as she uses the flashlight app to rifle through Post-it Notes and pens and binder clips. She gags at a travel-size Secret antiperspirant stick with some white deodorant crusted around the edges of the lid, and then shoves the drawer closed with a groan. "Come on, Ms. Marino. I know you got to be charging your phone during class!"

While Lena looks in the boxes and containers on top of the desk, I run my hands along the walls and bump into a lone charger plugged into a socket near the back of the room. Some student trying to charge a contraband phone on the down low, maybe grabbing the phone but forgetting the cord.

"Found one!" I call. Lena aims the light in my direction, and I lob it to her.

"Yasssss!" She swipes it from the air, but once she gets a look, her face crumples. "Apple? Aw, fail. I got an Android."

"Me too," I say, joining her by Ms. Marino's desk. "Androids get no love."

One corner of her mouth turns up. "That's the truth." She tosses the useless charger onto the desk. "Don't know if the power's on in here, anyway."

That is also the truth.

"Listen, you think maybe I could get a ride with your parents when they come get you? I need to get down to Seventh to meet my boyfriend."

"It's just my dad. And no. He's not around tonight."

I never used to imagine what my dad did on weekends. I figured he worked in his store, like he did the rest of the time. I've been living with him for nine weeks, so now I know. Every single weekend, he goes to his fishing cabin in the mountains. Nicky, his weekend manager, watches the store. Nicky's family owns the convenience market on Seventh. I guess they're my dad's friends. Considering they're the only people he's introduced me to, it seems like maybe they're his only friends. Nicky is a computer science major at Georgia Tech. Apparently, this summer he installed new software on the computer at the shop, so my dad made him manager. Without him, my dad wouldn't have been able to afford the upgrade, and without the upgrade, he wouldn't have been able to accept the credit cards with the chips in them. And then the store would bring in less money, and my dad would probably go bankrupt.

He pays Nicky way more than he can afford, but who else could he trust to manage the shop while he's off fishing? When I first moved, I thought maybe he'd hire me, but he said he couldn't swing paying anyone else. You'd think he'd be all about the idea of me having a job. Not only for the money, though I need that. But also because I have plenty of time for work. Practice used to take up all my time after school, and I had meets on the weekends. That's not part of my life anymore, so why not clock in somewhere that'll put some cash in my pocket?

My dad's being ridiculous. When I told him the wing place up by school was looking for a cashier, he said,

"Absolutely not. That's not the kind of place I want you spending time."

"What's that supposed to mean?" I asked. Yeah, the place was a little grungy, but I saw plenty of kids stopping in there after classes let out.

"This isn't Haverford, Campbell."

"That isn't news to me, Dad."

"How about this? There's a sandwich shop opening up by the store, run by a nice young couple. Hipsters, but decent people. Maybe in a few months, they'll be looking for some help. Then, I could keep an eye on you. Let's wait for that, okay?"

I rolled my eyes. The man has no sense of irony. I'm not allowed to work at a restaurant that's a twenty-minute walk from my house because it's too far away to keep an eye on me, but he's got no problem leaving me alone for the entire weekend so he can go fishing. I could be out roaming the neighborhood in the middle of the night while he's gone. Of course, I'm not. I've never gone farther than our mailbox while he's gone. But the point is, he doesn't know that.

Maybe he doesn't care.

He doesn't offer to take me with him to the cabin, and I don't ask to go. It's some dumpy little one-room shack, anyway.

The hipster sandwich shop job hasn't materialized yet. Of course.

I have no job, no practice, no parental supervision, no company, and no cash. My weekends revolve around hoping HGTV will do a *House Hunters International* marathon and waiting for my mom to FaceTime me. My friends call sometimes, though not as much as they did before they went back to school. I try not to think about the fun things that keep them from calling. Things I *was* doing with them four months ago, like playing foosball in Megan's parents basement and sneaking cans from her dad's beer fridge when we could. I deleted Instagram from my phone, because seeing all that stuff go on without me ate a giant hole in my heart.

"Boyfriend?" Lena asks.

"No."

"Best friend?"

I cross my arms and turn away.

An hour ago, Lena James had no idea what my name was, despite having a class together. She never bothered me—not like the girl who got in my face every day for the first three weeks of school, slamming lip gloss from my hands in the bathroom. Or the two who pulled my hair when they passed me in the stairwell. Lena's too wrapped up in herself for all that. She hangs with this group of kids that dress all hip-hop, cool enough to be in a music video, and Lena's the center of their attention. She's always making people laugh, calling everyone by name like she's their best friend. Even teachers. Whenever she's around, the Lena James Show is on and you can't help but watch. And the rest of the time, she's got her head down to her phone, texting so fast her fingers are a blur—I'm guessing with that boyfriend she mentioned.

She never noticed me before. How humiliating that the first thing she sees is that I have no friends. I can't imagine why she's getting in my business about this. I don't want to admit I'm waiting on a teacher for a ride, and I hate her a little for trying to make me.

"How are you getting home, though?" she demands. She steps up right next to me, getting into my space and forcing me to look at her. Her head tilts to the side, and her forehead is all wrinkled up. But she's not smirking. She's not laughing. She looks worried, actually.

There's no point in dodging. She's obviously not going to give up. "Ms. Marino was supposed to take me home," I say.

She stares at me. "Yeah, but now what are you gonna do?"

"Wait for her, I guess. Not like my dad is going to catch me if I break curfew."

"Girl, she ain't comin' back here."

A bolt of stress sizzles through me. No. That's not true. "Of course she is. She knows I'm waiting."

"Can't you hear them sirens?" Lena asks.

Actually, I do. A lot of them. I press my nose against

85

the window, craning my neck to see down the walkway toward the gym, but no matter how I turn, I can't see the football field. There are a few moving forms, but it's too dark to distinguish anything else. Are there more sirens? Am I imagining it, or are they getting louder?

"How do you think that's gonna end?" Lena taps the glass right by my face, startling me. "It ain't magically gonna calm down, and everybody go about their business. They'll start clearing people out soon. Marino's not coming back here. Even if she wanted to."

Oh, God.

No. She's wrong. Ms. Marino won't leave me. She'll find a way to get back here. She has to.

But those sirens. They're definitely louder. I figured all those police showing up would calm this down, but what if Lena's right? We're hardly going to go back to playing a football game after this.

I can't breathe. The bun I tied at the top of my head earlier to ward off the heat, stretches the skin beside my eyes too tight, giving me a headache. I reach up and work the elastic loose, letting my hair fall around my face to hide the tears that are gathering in the corners of my eyes. It's just stress, but I don't want to cry. I want everything to be normal again.

Except normal would be me and my mom living in Haverford, before her job cut her salary so much, we couldn't afford the mortgage, before Carlson's Hardware tanked so hard that my dad sued to reduce the amount of child support he had to pay, before my mom had to transfer to Venezuela or be fired. Normal would be me training for the 100-meter and trying to get scouts from UPenn to see me run at the state finals. Normal would not include the fight at the concession stand, this portable, or me being stranded by the teacher who was supposed to take me home.

Great, that train of thought became a runaway. I stopped crying, but I'm not calm. I'm just freaking out too hard for the tears to squeeze free.

How. Am. I. Going. To. Get. Home?

Beside me, Lena sighs. "Looks like we're both stuck. Guess it's a walk for us. Pops would kill me if he ever found out I'm doing this. Lucky thing he busy at church tonight."

What? I turn to her. "Walk?"

"We're not going through this again. Nobody coming to get you. What're you gonna do—spend the night here?"

I gulp. Right. Of course she's right. Sirens whine from the direction of the field. I can't stay here waiting for someone who's never going to come back for me. The walk home isn't that long—maybe twenty minutes. And at least we'd be together.

Wait. "But you said you're trying to get to Seventh. My house is kinda far from there."

"Yeah, but you in Grant Village, right?"

I blink. Besides the secretary who helped my dad register me, Lena James might be the only person at McPherson who's aware of where I live. A flutter of grateful excitement kicks up in my belly, but I squelch it. So she paid a little attention to me. It won't last. People's attention never holds. "Yes, that's right."

"Where your house at?"

"I live on Taylor Street," I say. "But I don't know my way around very well."

"I do. That's not too far from where I stay. How about you walk down to Seventh with me and meet my boyfriend? He got a car. He could give you a ride home."

I frown. I don't know Lena all that well, and her boyfriend is a total stranger. He definitely doesn't go to McPherson. My mother would go nuclear if she found out I got into some strange guy's car.

"Look, I'm trying to be nice to you, but if you too afraid, then you can hide here—by yourself—for the rest of this night."

My fear spikes. She's going to leave. I can't stay here. I can't.

"Fine!" The shout rings around the empty room, shrill enough to startle me. God, I have got to dial it down. "I mean, thanks for offering a ride. I'll come with you."

Lena stops in the doorway, and my stomach churns. What if she changed her mind? What if I insulted her?

She's got a better blank face than the guys my dad watches on the World Series of Poker. I need to get out of here, and she's offering to go with me, and instead of saying yes, I'm shouting at her. God, I'm absurd.

Before I can get any more words out, Lena grabs her purse from the floor by the desk and marches to the door. "Let's go," she says.

I scramble after her.

We encounter a few people on our way back to the field. They're all running. Running away from the place we're heading. My stomach starts jumping around once I realize that, but we keep going. The walk to the gym only takes a minute or two. I round the corner of the building and slam into a wall of noise and lights. I thought the sirens sounded loud inside the classroom. I thought what we walked out of thirty minutes ago was as bad as it could get.

I was wrong.

The power is still out, but the stadium isn't dark anymore. Emergency lights strobe, washing the scene blue-red-black, blue-red-black, blue-red-black. A swarm of bodies pulsates around the field, people reeling and staggering, flooding forward, swaying back, swirling endlessly. Almost like a party, if the lights were a different color. If there was music, instead of sirens and—oh, God—rotors? I squint up, using my palm to shield my eyes from the sweeping floodlights, and see two helicopters hovering overhead,

adding to the noise and confusion. Police? Or maybe a
news station?

The parking lot swarms with emergency vehicles, and
the stadium is full of police officers. An army of them.
Every cop in the city must have descended on McPherson.
From the east side of the field, Central Avenue, an ambulance screams into the parking lot. Two paramedics slam
open the doors, jump down, pulling the gurney after them.

I can't think about what that gurney is for. I can't think
about the gunshots.

I look away from the parking lot as fast as I can, my
throat closing up. It's too noisy. Too overwhelming.

"We shouldn't have come outside," I breathe.

But we did.

Lena was right. Ms. Marino's not coming back for me.
She'll never get back here, assuming she remembers me at
all. I have to get home. Twenty minutes, I remind myself,
straight down Central. I can make it. *We* can. It's right
across the parking lot. The lot that's currently choked by
cop cars and fire engines and ambulances, teeming with
police and first responders.

Thank God. At least we don't have to walk through the
actual field. That would be ridiculously dangerous.

I start forward—and straight into the arm Lena has
flung in front of me. I try to sidestep, but she grabs me,
holds me back. Not just holds me—nearly drags me off

my feet. I turn to look at her and see, for the first time, her pretty features twisted in panic.

No. *Fear.*

"We can't go there."

I look from her wide, rolling eyes to the war zone before me. "But we have to."

"You seein' what I am? How we gonna get through there?"

"We'll go straight to the parking lot. It's full of cops, we'll be—"

"You want to go *to* the cops? You must be playin'!"

She's holding my arm so tight, her nails dig into my skin. "Lena, how else are we going to get to Central?"

"I said no! I'm not gettin' anywhere near them po po."

"They're not going to bother us. We didn't do anything."

"They ain't gonna bother you, maybe! They look at you and see a poodle. They look at me and all they see is a pit bull."

Pit bull? *Lena?* I don't understand what she's talking about, but she lets me go and wraps her arms around herself. Her knees lock, drawing her up straight, but she's not still. She's shaking. Freaking out harder than she did in the concession stand when they were shooting. Bullets didn't make her shake, but this does.

Only trouble is, I have no idea what else to do.

A figure comes jogging toward us, shrouded in darkness, feet slapping the pavement, getting closer. I press into the wall of the gym, plucking at Lena's arm to pull her with me. Maybe if I get her away from those lights, she'll think more clearly.

"Lena, come on," I say. "It'll only take a minute to get to Central."

"Can't go down Central," a very-nearby voice calls.

I shriek. Lena presses closer to me. The jogger is right by us now, and he pauses for a second. "Police blockaded Central," he pants. "Can't go down that way. Only way out of here is First."

We both cower against the gym wall—but the jogger doesn't stop for long, and he doesn't come any closer. In fact, he veers away from us, away from the portables, toward the side entrance to the school. The *other* side. The non-football-field side. The side I never use.

My stomach swoops into my shoes. First Avenue?

No. No, no, no, no. First passes right through Tillman Park. My dad drilled into me from the day I moved here that I'd better not ever get near there. Grant Village, his neighborhood, is a little run down. There's some abandoned houses, some boarded-up businesses, and too many overgrown yards and empty lots where guys who are my age but definitely don't go to my school sit on upside-down paint buckets, passing joints.

Tillman Park, which takes over north of Grant Village all the way to Highway 20, is different. The kind of different that makes people drive through going fifty in a thirty zone.

"We are so screwed!" Lena breathes.

We're trapped. We have no way to get out of here. My lungs don't seem to be working properly. I can't push enough air through them, can't inflate them.

"Pops is definitely gonna kill me for walking down First," Lena says.

I blanch. "What? We're not going through there."

"How else we gonna get out of here? You heard that boy. Central's blockaded."

"We can't! I don't know my way home. We'll get lost. And Central goes through the ghetto!"

"*Ghetto?* Don't worry. Don't nobody want yo' skinny ass in the ghetto," Lena snaps. I flinch, because I didn't mean that. Whatever insulted her is not what I meant. I open my mouth to tell her—what? I'm sorry? I don't know. She cuts me off with a palm in my face. "Listen, we'll cut over to Seventh as soon as we can and meet up with Black. It's a few blocks. Anyway, we won't be by ourselves. Other people headed down that way."

She's right. The guy who told us about the blockade has faded into the darkness, but he was definitely headed that way. There are others too, a couple of small groups. All fleeing the school out the side entrance.

"First?" I whisper.

I have never walked down First Avenue in my life. It's not safe. A light from one of the helicopters sweeps over us. Deep voices boom through bullhorns. I peek around the corner of the gym one more time, my gaze traveling from the still-raging fight to the parking lot full of police. I look back into Lena's frightened face, red and blue and white lights flickering in her eyes.

She's as afraid of that crowd of cops as I am of First.

Suddenly, my anxiety seems extreme. She's suggesting we walk a couple of blocks through a bad neighborhood. I'm insisting we plow through a riot.

Tillman Park can't be that bad. With Lena, I ought to be safe. Safe enough for one night. If we walk fast, we might get to her boyfriend faster than we would walking down Central.

"Okay," I say, sounding shaky in my own ears. Wondering if she notices. "First."

Lena nods. "First."

She sounds as nervous as me.

12

LENA

First Ave

Once we get down south of Highway 20, I'll feel like I can breathe again. I don't even like being over here on this part of First Ave on a regular day, because this is where all those abandoned buildings are where stuff be happening to girls. And this is the corner where LaShunda's cousin Noel got her new car jacked, and they didn't realize her baby was still in the back seat. But I bet I'll recognize somebody hanging around, so I'll be straight.

We cut through the Citgo and I look for familiar faces, but I don't see nobody. There's not as many people walking out of the school as I thought there'd be either. Maybe a whole lotta people getting arrested.

"Is there a party I wasn't invited to or did the gas station run out of beer to sell?" I'm trying to joke, but my chest gets a little tighter and I walk faster.

Campbell looks over at me like she's confused. I shake my head. And then I see her feet. Say what you want about white girl, but she smart enough to be wearing tennis shoes.

"Girl, I'm a little jealous of your kicks. My feet killin' me. I'm tempted to take off my shoes."

"Oh, no, don't do that!" Her eyes get big. "You'd get tetanus or something."

"Way I feel," I say. "Might be worth it."

There's some people out on the streets, like always in this part of the neighborhood. Not really the people I hang around with, but I recognize a few of them. Like this one, a gentleman we all call Happy, with a thick mustache wearing combat boots, purple pants, and a fitted halter top walking across the street from us. He a regular around here, and for some reason, I kinda like him.

Happy stops when he sees us and looks me over, like he always do. "Love those sandals, girl," he says. He points at my feet and then at my face. "Cannot deny those sandals."

"Yasssssss," I say. "Happy, you know I cannot pass on a fierce pair of sandals."

"Where'd you find them at?"

Oh no. I don't wanna answer that, 'cuz he will go off the moment I tell him where. He and LaRue beef because Happy says he's more fabulous than she is, and she won't own that. But Happy sees through all lies.

"Uh, LaRue's."

"I'm surprised that LaRue, who is a *fashion don't*, got anything right. Maybe I might have to grace her shop with my presence one more time after all." Lord, no. LaRue would drop dead on the spot if Happy walked back in her store, but I'm here for it. "Sis, what are you doin' over here on my streets? You don't normally be in the Park."

"Trust me, I am on my way out of here," I say. "Tryna get to a ride."

"Okay, well, y'all get on outta here quick. The air ain't right tonight."

I shiver. Happy walks these streets all day, and if he's sayin' it's bad…

He heads off in the other direction, and in another block, we come up on one of the houses that always freak me out with boarded-over windows and broken furniture in the yard. That's where all the J's and drunks be at. And I am not trying to mess with them. So what we're not going to do is pass by that house. That house is a reminder of why I don't ever come up to Tillman Park. I was feeling okay, talking to Happy, but now, not so much.

"C'mon," I say. "Let's cross the street."

Campbell follows me to the other side. At least this way, if a junkie do run out, I'll have time to see 'em coming and run or find a brick to bust 'em in the head. To make matters worse, I have to keep my head to the ground because of all the broken glass, like a trail of bread crumbs leading right back to that trap house.

Maybe that's why we get all the way to the next street before I notice a homeless dude I ain't never seen before. He's there on the corner, shouting to himself, and I don't recognize him. Aw, man. I call myself getting away from this type of junkie, not walking right into a conversation with one! I start to walk faster as we cross toward him. Campbell stays with me.

"Aye, you gotta dollar I could borrow?" he hollers at us when we reach his side.

I grab Campbell's elbow and hustle her forward. "Borrow—is this man for real?" I whisper to her. "How he gon' borrow it when he ain't gon' see me to return it?"

But we gone and done it, because he starts following us. "You see me," he says. "You see me all the time!"

I speed up. After a minute, I just know dude gotta be gone, but I hear footsteps. I raise my hand and pretend to push my hair out of my face, but really, I'm sneaking a peek over my shoulder. Oh. My. God. He is still there. I slide my arm through Campbell's and pull her closer. She look at me, her eyes huge. We need to get away from his stinky self, but the faster we walk, the faster he walks. There is nobody around, except him, which is not okay. For the first time all night, I can't guess what's coming next.

"Now we got some crackhead following us," I whisper to Campbell. "He prolly the one started that fire that burnt down the highway."

Behind us, he grumbles, "Do you know what I'd do with a pretty girl like you?"

My chest tightens. We have to get out of here. Please, God, let him go away.

Then he goes from mumbling under his breath to shouting, scaring the heck out of us.

"Why you running away from me? You think that white girl make you better than me?"

At the sound of his scratchy voice, Campbell squeezes me tighter and pushes me forward. "Come on, come on!"

"You too good to speak to me, you bougie little bitch?" he demands. "You got money in that purse!"

He lunges and grabs my arm.

My heart drops into my shoes. All I can think to do is snatch away, but his grip is too strong. My eyes fill with water. I can't get away from this guy. He's pulling on me hard. But Campbell's not letting go.

She yanks on me and he yanks on me, and Campbell suddenly shouts, "Stop!"

He look so surprised she did that, he lets go. She pulls me away from his grip, and the two of us take off as fast as we can. And look at Campbell. She can fly! I'm flying too. We don't look back. My chest is on fire. When we get to the next block, I glance back to see if we've lost him, and I hope we have.

"Campbell," I push out, breathing heavy.

She stops, face all flushed and puts her hand on her chest.

"Who knew you was a gangsta?" I gasp. "That man had me like he was gonna run off with me, but he wasn't no match for the Campbell Soup!"

She giggles, while she's bent over, panting and all. "I can't believe I did that!"

"Believe it. You whooped a homeless man ass!"

Though she's shaking her head, we're both laughing.

"Girl, you always move like your ass is on fire or just when a homeless dude's chasin' you?"

"I ran track at my old school. I'm a sprinter."

"Yeah, you are. You on the track team here? 'Cuz if you're not, you should be."

Her laughter stops. "I tried out, but I, uh, got cut."

She sounds real sad, and I feel bad for making her remember. My smile fades, and I nod at her. "Anyway, thanks, Campbell Soup."

I don't know what else to say.

13

CAMPBELL

First Avenue
North of Tillman Park

We're both winded. I spend so much time looking over my shoulder, making sure that guy—any guy—isn't behind us, that I trip twice. He's not, but I'm still buzzing. My arms and legs feel full of Fourth of July sparklers, flickering and crackling. On fire. Every sound from every house we pass, every barking dog, the sirens still streaming back the other way, all send me jumping. As the dark settles around us, the sparklers going off inside me mutate into exploding bottle rockets.

"Jesus, we have to get out of here! This was the most unsafe move I've ever made."

"Relax," Lena says. "That was a bit much, but we almost outta here. A few more streets and then we'll be back in Grant Village."

"No!" I shout and then flinch and look around. How careless am I, attracting more attention to us? I'm practically begging for another scary guy to attack us. "We cannot keep walking around like this. Hey, call your boyfriend. Tell him to come get us. We'll—we'll hide out on someone's porch or something until he gets here."

"Yeah, no. Not doin' that."

"Why not?"

"You don't understand," she says. "I do not demand he up and change his entire schedule. It does not work like that. Black can't break away just because I said I need a ride."

"Well, maybe your grandpa?"

"No, Campbell." I open my mouth, but she flings a hand out, palm up. "Ain't nobody got time to be coming and cleaning up after me. Everybody around here got somebody to be responsible for—I'm lucky since I only got me to worry about. I figure life out for myself. Anyway, Miss Somebody Needs to Save Us, why you don't call us an Uber? Black'll give you the cash for half when we get to Seventh."

My throat closes up. Like everyone has a credit card they can use to Uber all around and a boyfriend who'll pay for the rides. I have a five-dollar bill in my pocket and the food in my dad's fridge to last the weekend. If I wanted dinner at the concession stand, I couldn't have afforded to buy chips, a soda, and a hot dog. I'd have had to pick my favorite two out of three.

I didn't spend much time with my dad after my parents split. The typical two weeks every summer until I got old enough to ask to stay with my mom, so I could join a summer track club. I was probably eleven or twelve the last time I visited, but I knew there was a difference between his dusty little shop and the Home Depot. So I wasn't massively shocked when I moved here this fall to see he's barely paying his bills. That he doesn't always pay every bill every month. My mom's only transferred me money once and not that much. She says Caracas is more expensive to live in than she thought. Or maybe this is her way of getting back at my dad for all those years the child support checks bounced.

No. I won't think like that about her. She's doing her best, like she always does. She might get overwhelmed sometimes by her job, but she never lets two days go by without calling, and she remembers all the details I tell her about my classes. That's the best part about my mom. She takes whatever you tell her so seriously, like you're sharing state secrets. That hasn't changed, though I'm telling her details across an international telephone wire instead of across the dinner table.

And she promised she's saving up for a plane ticket so I can spend Christmas with her. It's only a few months to wait.

No way am I telling Lena any of that. I cross my arms and look away. "I don't have the app downloaded. Besides, no Uber is coming in *here* to get us."

"And why's that, Campbell?" she asks, sounding sharp.

I roll my eyes. Like she doesn't know. She wants to make me feel bad for being jumpy, but it's not my fault. I'm desperate and my knees are shaking and we're still in freaking Tillman Park and so I keep vomiting words. "How about you knock on someone's door and ask for help?"

"Me?" She glares. "You think I can post up on some stranger's porch, and they'll be fine with that?"

"You must know someone who lives around here that we can ask for help."

"I sure as hell do not." Lena stops and stares at me, her eyes cold, her mouth pinched. "Where do you think you are?"

"The ghetto," I cry. "And I don't want to be here anymore."

"First," she snarls, "*ghetto* is a person. The *hood* is a place. Second, you walk around here like you don't live here."

I don't, I want to shout. "What's that supposed to mean?"

"You wanna talk about this?" she yells. "Fine. Let's talk about the fact that you expected I got friends here. Or the fact that you assumed I would be safe knocking on a stranger's door in Tillman Park? Which we have established is the hood. You wanna tell me why you thought that? Couldn't be because I'm black, could it?"

"No," I say, my voice wobbling. "I—you—you've lived here longer than me. I don't know the neighborhood."

"'Cuz you ain't tried to. Exactly like some rich, white

bitch moving in and trying to change the place instead of living in it like it is!"

"I'm not rich."

"Please. Your daddy own a store down Seventh, right?"

I'm surprised she's aware of that. She acts like she knows nothing about me. Or maybe she just acts like she doesn't care.

"That doesn't make me rich, okay?"

"Sure, yeah. I'm crying for you. Daddy couldn't afford to buy you the newest iPhone, could he? Had to wait 'til all your friends already got one and you was the last. Boo-hoo, poor little, rich white girl."

"I might not walk around with a chip on my shoulder talking about how hard my life is, but that doesn't mean it's all rainbows and unicorns either."

I squint. I hope she thinks that's my mad face and not that I'm holding back tears. This moment transports me back home, to the times when everyone would make plans that cost a lot of money and figured I wouldn't have a problem coming up with the cash to join. My stomach clenches. The anger between us swells like a balloon I want to stick a pin in and explode, but if I'm honest, I don't want to either. "I'm not rich, Lena, and I can't help that I'm white. You don't get to blame me for something I can't control."

"Why not, Becky? You people blame me for being born black every single day!"

105

"That's not true. That's an excuse for poor choices."

"You wanna repeat that?" She sounds stone cold.

A nervous tingle starts in my toes, replacing the flash of anger that made me say such a thoughtless thing. "Never mind," I mutter.

"You ain't walkin' away from that. Oh, hell, no. Is it a bad choice to get in an elevator? Or how 'bout walk into a store?"

"What are you talking about?"

"I get in an elevator and people clutch they purses like I'm gonna steal from them. Why you think they do that, huh?"

I open my mouth to respond, and I get stuck. I have seen that happen. I don't want to admit this, but I do get nervous when a black guy gets in an elevator with me. Not because he's black, though. Just when it's a big guy and a small space. That's all. But suddenly, I wonder.

Suddenly, I'm not sure.

"And how 'bout in a store? You get followed around like you gonna take the whole store? No, you don't. You a rich white girl, and you ain't never gonna know what any of that's like, and let me tell you somethin' else. You lucky you only said that to me. You say some racist nonsense like that to anyone else, and they gonna beat yo ass."

I close my mouth, grind my teeth together. I want to tell her I am not racist. I want to say she's wrong about me.

106

But she swings around and starts walking—fast. Despite her impractical shoes, which must be killing her, she's on the move, and if I don't hurry, I'll get left behind. And I definitely do not want to be left behind here. I don't want to face her either, so I lag, staying two strides behind.

Fortunately, Lena was right, and we are only a couple of streets away from Grant Village. As the neighborhood transitions, the houses have fewer boarded-up windows and graffiti tags and more FOR SALE signs decorate the yards of fancy new construction homes. And churches start to pop up. Lots and lots of churches. We pass three in the first two streets. In Haverford, the nearest church had been a fifteen-minute drive from my house. Here, churches are almost as common as mailboxes: Baptist, African Methodist Episcopal, Seventh Day Adventist, nondenominational. They're all in these little brick buildings that look like they might be someone's home. Like you could walk in and right behind the sanctuary, you'd find a kitchen with a stove and a refrigerator.

For all I know, that's what you would find. I've never been inside any of them.

I think of what Lena said, how I walk around like I don't live here. How I'm looking at these churches like I'm a tourist. How I wouldn't be able to find my dad's house from here. My whole body goes hot, like someone's dipping me in lava.

At the next intersection, First officially changes names

to MLK Boulevard and becomes residential. And the air starts to smell. Stink, really, like there's a broken sewer line. I fan my hand in front of my nose and try not to breathe. I don't have to wonder if the stench bothers Lena, though.

"Ewwwwww," she cries. "Smells like the bathroom when Pops has a sit-down after too much banana pudding at the church dinner."

I snort. Maybe she wasn't trying to be funny, but it's *so* true. These days, I share a one-bathroom house with my father, and I have endured exactly the smell she's talking about. For my dad, the frozen chicken wings he makes when he watches football are the culprit.

Thinking about that gets me laughing. "Oh, my God. What is it about guys?"

In unison, we say, "They stink!"

We both giggle, and I look at her, my stomach aching. I fight with the tangle our conversation has made of my thoughts, wanting to say something more. Something better.

"Hey, listen—"

My phone dings.

"Black!" Lena cries. She lunges at me, digs into my pocket, and grabs my phone.

I don't have time to tell her that's not the sound of a text message.

Her face crumples as she reads the notification from one of my apps. "Your crops are dying—water them."

"Lena," I say, stretching out a hand toward her to—
what? Pat her arm? Take the phone back? I have to be the
last person she wants to hear from at this moment.

Confirming my suspicion, she jerks away. "Shut up,
okay?"

She slides my phone into her shorts pocket. I don't
have the right words to respond, so I follow as she starts
down the street.

14

LENA

MLK and Pine Grove
North of Tillman Park

Ugh.

This girl. I thought we were on the same page. Clearly, we're not. She can keep her Uber rides to herself. She's definitely got that app, and she just don't want to share. What does she think is gonna happen—the driver gonna one-star her for being in this neighborhood? For the record, I may not be from Tillman Park, but plenty of people around here just be workin' hard, tryna live their best life.

We need to head down to Seventh and go our separate ways, so I can be free of her and her crap. We're only a couple blocks from Pine Grove Street, so I speed up. But that makes me more nervous because I notice how alone I am. Usually, there's some people outside on their way to a bar or a porch party. I don't like how this feels. Happy was right. Somethin' off about tonight.

"What time is it?" Campbell asks.

I roll my eyes, but I guess I have to answer. I do got her phone. "Oh wow, ten thirty already," I say, lighting up the screen for a minute. "This 'bout the longest amount of time you ever spent with a black girl, right?"

She catches up to me, but she won't look at me. "No!"

I throw my palms up, like, *chill out, sista.* "I ain't judgin'. Not like I hang around with no white people. I was curious is all."

Campbell goes quiet for a second. "Yeah, I guess so. There weren't that many African American kids at my old school, and they mostly hung around with each other."

"Yeah," I say. "That's what I figured."

I don't know how to feel about this girl at this point. On one hand, she been a rider. She held me down against the homeless old man, and she been rolling with me on this whole trip, not asking too many questions. That don't change the fact that when she does talk, she keep saying ignorant stuff.

I ain't surprised old homeless dude didn't like me walking around the neighborhood with her. Black people around here ain't really messing with white folks these days. I ain't surprised by what happened at the school either. This really wasn't no time to be putting us in no competitive situation against the kids from that rich suburban school. It was all over Instagram last month, like Caleb said, their football players dressed up in blackface for a party and weren't even suspended.

And that ain't all that's happened. A few weeks back, those paramedics wouldn't go into the projects and they let that little boy die. Then, they reelected that racist governor who called us "colored" in a speech. And then, when we demonstrated because that ain't no way to talk, and blocked the highway, they arrested like forty people and called us thugs. Not to mention all the cops around the country acting like it's open season on black folks.

When I look up, we're at Pine Grove. That homeless dude threw me all the way off. Up ahead, that's where my nosy cousin Marcus and his scrubs at. Oh man, these guys. I should have known I was gonna run into him out here. Ain't got nowhere better to be on a Friday night than an empty lot and not so much as a tricycle between 'em to get nowhere else either. He's gonna slow us down, but it's kinda nice to see his face. At least with him around, some homeless bum's not gonna jump out at me.

"I gotta go holler at my cousin," I say.

Campbell eyes Marcus and his friends. She knots her hair into a bun, but her hands are shaking.

"Hey, Campbell Soup. You good?"

"I'm fine."

Her words do not match up with her face. "Listen, this big-top circus crew might look shady, but don't worry," I say. "They're all soft as gummy bears. That one over there— the big guy? Look at his arm when we get up close. He got a Hufflepuff tattoo."

She snorts. "Seriously?"

"You'll see." I smile. "Whatever we do, though, we gotta be quick. I do not want Marcus to start preaching."

I step through the opening, careful of the chain link that's twisted like a Fruit Roll-Up, and I walk over to them. "'Sup?" I say, letting out a sigh.

"NaNa, what's good, lil cuz?" Marcus says. "I just had asked Pops about you."

Asked Pops about me means, as usual, he was trying to get all up in my business for whatever reason. "What're you asking about me for?"

"I'm lookin' out for you, NaNa," he says. "I always have and I always will."

"I don't need you to," I say. "I got my situation under control."

Marcus's friend Malik chuckles. Malik annoys me because he's cute and he's fully aware I used to have a little bit of a crush on him. But that was way before Black, so no reason for him to be big-headed. "Don't hurt the boy, now," Malik says. "We know you got this."

I glare at him. I ain't gonna respond to that. Cricket

114

pipes up, holding out a leg with a brand new pair of Nikes so fresh out the box, they don't have a scuff on them.

"Hey, NaNa. Whatchu think of my new kicks?"

"She thinks it's a good thing you standin' on that bench, short stack, or she wouldn't be able to see 'em." That's Sheldon, who's always got something to say.

"Don't listen to them, Cricket," I say. "They jealous of your style. You always killin' it."

All them boys go *oooooh* like a bunch of fools, and that makes Cricket pop off.

"I don't need to be tall," he says. "A punch in the nuts hurts as bad as a punch in the face."

Pee Wee laughs. "Yeah, you are just about nut-level!"

I hold my hand up in his face and turn to Cricket. "Haters gonna hate, Cricket. You keep doin' you. That's what I do."

"And what're you doing down here tonight, NaNa?" Sheldon says.

"Me and my girl headed to Seventh."

Marcus looks confused and surprised all together. From the corner of my eye, Campbell does too, but praise God, she don't mention Black.

"Your girl? Since when is this your kinda girl?" Marcus asks.

My cousin makes me so mad.

"What are you trying to say, Marcus? You sayin' I'm not

good enough to hang with Campbell or Campbell's not good enough to hang with me? Which one?"

"I'm not sayin' either one," he says. "I'm asking why all of a sudden you're walkin' around with Becky. And as a matter of fact, did y'all come through Tillman Park?"

"Tillman Park is nothing compared to what we been through together. That was the only way we could go after what happened at the school."

Marcus looks from me to Campbell and back, and I can tell he gettin' upset. "You were at the school? When they were shooting?"

Oh. My. God. I talk too much! I better think real fast, to get him off this without him having more to say. "When we were there, it was just a fight. We got out of there before anything too wild popped off." Lord, let Campbell remain on mute. I hope she don't blow up my spot and wind him up. "We're on our way to Joe's."

"Joe's on a Friday night?" Marcus says. "What's down there for you?"

Malik jumps in. "Black."

I glare at him, but at least he's talking and not Campbell. "You so busy mindin' my business 'cuz you ain't got none of your own, huh, Malik?"

"NaNa. You ain't meeting Black, is you?" Marcus asks, his voice all deep and serious.

I could lie, but why should I have to? My relationship

with Black ain't none of his business. "And so what if I am, Marcus?"

"I keep telling you he ain't nothin', and I don't like to call a black man a nigga, but that's a nigga."

"You don't know him well enough to call him nothin'!" I say.

"Man, I'm too familiar with him and those dudes he's tryna be down with," Marcus says. "And that ain't for you. Not one of them fools gon' elevate yo mind, lil sister."

Here we go. "You might've heard some BS about his crew," I say. "But that ain't him."

"We are only as good as the five people around us," Marcus says, up in his pulpit now. "Mostly because we share the same value system as those five. So he with them, then he made a choice on livin' like them. He can be an eagle, but if he choose to flock with pigeons, he gon' have pigeon ways."

Dang, I'm mad at myself for not avoiding this corner. I take a look around—broken glass, a raggedy bunch of furniture thrown together for them to sit on. These fools done made a living room situation out of an abandoned lot. Like, who does that? But Bootleg Hotep wanna sit up here and lecture me on who bae choose to hang with?

"Yeah, 'cuz this is a regular presidential cabinet you kickin' it with?" I point at Pee Wee, the worst of the lot. He's on his sixth job this year and got two baby mamas to support. "The way I see it, you ain't in a position to judge nobody."

"Okay, lil cuz, you got all the answers today. But I'm telling you, that cat is gonna be your demise. A no-good man has been the end of so many women. Don't be a statistic."

"I am gonna be a statistic. They gotta do statistics on rich people too. We gon' be right up there with Jay-Z and Beyoncé, Will and Jada, Michelle and Barack. Watch and see."

I'm so tired of this conversation, and enough time has been wasted. I'm ready to go. All I need is a little interruption, because Marcus ain't gonna give up no time soon. I wish LaShunda was with me. She would have already come over here and stopped this bull, made up an excuse as to why we have to move. LaShunda's good like that, and Marcus an'nem don't mess with her. I look over at Campbell and give her a long glare. I hope she catches the hint to step up.

15

CAMPBELL

MLK Boulevard and Pine Grove

The nerves in my legs crawl, shifting me from foot to foot. I can't settle in one spot. I'm not part of this conversation Lena's having with these guys. These guys I've driven past but never gotten near.

A half dozen of them sit on buckets and a bench they've constructed out of cinder blocks and rotten lumber. There's an old kitchen chair with a wicker seat that's sagging under the weight of its occupant, who sits on it backward, poking his fingers through the torn spots. The three guys on the bench pass a blunt, the musty smell sharp in my nostrils from way over here. A tall, skinny guy with the longest dreads I've ever seen holds a cell phone streaming music. From the way Lena argues with him, I'm guessing that's Marcus.

A bunch of guys skulking around at night in a

fenced-off lot should be keeping quiet, shouldn't they? They're not supposed to be here, right? I glance around, worried someone's going to come over and…and do what?

What am I so anxious about?

No one in this lot is hiding. The music is loud. They're all loud, calling and laughing, talking, dancing a minute ago. Smoking right out in public. They have no fear the cops might come by any minute. Maybe I'm the only who's freaked out here. Maybe I'm the only one who needs to be. That homeless man's terrible taunts and Marcus's comments about me not being Lena's kind of girl.

They don't want me around, that's clear, though they haven't said anything to me directly. They're pretending I'm not here, which is fine, since I'm pretending I'm not here too. If I draw attention to myself, we'll all have to stop acting like this isn't happening.

Lena's conversation with Marcus is getting intense. Her hands are planted on her hips, one set of those clawlike nails drumming fast on the pocket of her shorts. He's way taller than her, and she's got her neck craned so she can look into his face.

I stand there, trying not to squirm whenever anyone glances my way, gripping the straps of my backpack tightly enough that it hurts. I think my hands might have frozen there. I'm considering trying to loosen my grip finger by finger, wondering if anyone will notice me being awkward, when Lena looks at me. As her eyes meet mine, I can read her mind.

Get me out of here.

The clarity of the plea, beamed directly from her brain to mine, drags words out of me. "Lena, we should go."

The voice shakes, but it's loud and rings over the talking and the music, and it's mine.

Oh, my God. What if I misunderstood what she wanted from me? What if she didn't want me to intervene?

One of the guys from the bench shouts, "Where you runnin' off to, Jennifer Lawrence? She talkin' here."

My face is on fire.

"Shut up, Pee Wee!" Lena snaps. "We goin'."

"Hold up, hold up," Marcus says. "After I just told you you can't trust that boy, you gonna run off to meet him? 'Cuz your little friend told you to?"

"Marcus, mind yo business." Lena sashays over to me and links her arm through mine. "Anyway, I'm meetin' Black because he gonna give me a ride to Campbell house, okay?"

Wait. What? She's coming to my house?

Marcus glances from Lena to me with a frown on his face.

"Where you think you gon' find him?" Malik asks. "He ain't got the balls to stick around no serious situation."

Lena points a shimmery nail at him. I recognize this pose. She's getting worked up. I wonder if the guys feel nervous. I do.

"We left the *situation* back up at the school, you fool," she says.

"Naw, streets is hot all over the city right now. My cousin's down by Joe's. He text me it's turnin' up."

"What you mean, Malik?"

"My cuz be down at the Icarus right next to Joe's." He holds up a cell phone. "He says somebody had planned a march, and some folks on the opposite side showed up, and those two do not go together."

"Lemme see!" Lena leans over and snatches his phone.

I blanch. I can't believe she did that. Wait, actually, I can. She has a serious phone-grabbing problem. She skims a finger over the screen, her eyes intent.

"Chill, shorty," Malik says, reaching for the phone.

She twists away, and there's a minute where Lena's reading the phone and Malik is trying to grab it from her, leaning way off the bench to get at her. He reaches too far and tumbles from his seat, landing in a heap at Lena's feet. The other guys burst into loud laughter. Lena looks up, and she laughs too. When she does, Marcus reaches over and plucks the phone from her hands.

"NaNa, I know Pops taught you better than to grab a man's phone."

"I ain't see no men here, just a buncha boys hanging out on a corner." Lena flings her hair behind her shoulder and steps away from Malik, who's scrambling to his feet with an angry scowl. For a second, I think he's going to grab Lena, but Marcus puts a hand to his chest and pushes him away. "If Seventh was so turnt up, we'd've heard. Black ain't say nothin' like that."

"That's 'cuz he prolly ain't there no more," Marcus says.

Anger curdles Lena's features. "He's waiting on me!" But the arm she has through mine spasms. Suddenly I get her panic over getting to Black. She isn't sure he's going to be there waiting for her. She isn't sure at all. I'm not surprised. He sounds like a jerk, but I am shocked that Lena James is chasing after a guy who isn't chasing back.

"Campbell ain't got no messages about that neither," she says.

They look at me. Oh, God. All those faces. Expecting me to speak up. There's no one in the world who would have told me what's going on down on Seventh Avenue. Lena's got to be aware of that.

"Uh…"

"Ain't that right, Campbell?" Lena widens her eyes and cocks her head with this aggressive twitch.

I fumble for my phone, which Lena has. My hands go to my pockets, patting awkwardly for a minute, and then I shake my head. "Yeah, uh, nope. I haven't heard about that."

There's no way any of them believe me, but Lena's features relax and she offers me a tiny smile that makes me feel like I won a trophy.

"See, Marcus? You worried for nothin'."

"Don't be a fool, NaNa. You walkin' into trouble when you oughta go home." He frowns for a second and then tips a couple of fingers at his friends. "Matter of fact, that's where you need to be, and I'm gonna take you there."

Lena's face gets tight and her eyes roll. She seems more annoyed than she has all night. But behind the annoyance, there's real worry. "I am not goin' home. And you must be drunk if you think you can tell me what to do, Marcus. You ain't my daddy."

"No, and I ain't yo pops neither. He know what you get into with that loser?"

"If he mysteriously find out about me and Black, yo mama gonna find out I ran into you messin' around this lot with these fools."

I watch their argument like a tennis match, swiveling back and forth. I can't imagine talking to anyone around here in Lena's sassy tone of voice, let alone him. Maybe he is her cousin, but his *don't play with me* vibe radiates more powerfully than hers.

"I told you, I'm going to Seventh and you can't stop me."

"Hey, Marcus, you gonna let your little cuz walk herself down there on a Friday night?" one guy calls. "Ain't no place for a couple chicks on they own." That sounds nice, like he's looking out for us, but from the mockery in his tone, he's goading Lena's cousin. It works.

Marcus stands and tosses the phone back to Malik. "No. I'm gonna head on down to Seventh with you, to meet up with Mr. Black and have a little chat with him about all the time he has been spending around my cousin."

"Oh no, you ain't," Lena screeches. "Let's go, Campbell."

She pulls on me, and I can't quite get myself turned around fast enough. Lena's marching away, sliding back through the fence, dragging me along. Marcus comes after us in long, jogging steps. His friends are shouting, catcalling. I don't really grasp what they're saying, but sounds like they're making fun. Lena waves a hand behind her, and if I don't hurry, she'll dismiss me, like she dismissed them. And I'd be left behind. My heart starts to race.

I hurry to keep up.

16

LENA

Pine Grove Ave

"I cannot let Marcus get to Black!"

"What?" Campbell whispers.

I glance at her, like *what are you talking about*, and after a second I realize I said that out loud. And then, I decide I might as well tell her.

"Marcus and Black don't get along too well. The tension's been building for a bit. And then last month, we was at the block party for Labor Day, and me and Black was chillin' and havin' a good time, and here come Marcus, pulling his usual big brother act. Only, he did that in front of everybody, so of course Black had to clap back. Next thing, they was punching each other. Ms. Johnson, this neighbor, she was about to call the police, so you know it was serious. Big Baby had to break them up, because Black don't need any marks on his pretty face, and Marcus don't need to be violating his probation."

Campbell stares at me, her mouth all wide. "Are you serious?"

"Girl, yassss. Everybody says Black is a thunderstorm when he wanna be."

"Whoa." She blinks like she can't take all this in. "What happened then?"

"Well, then Pops showed up at the party, and me and Black had to take off. I knew Pops would take Marcus's side. He don't never give Black a fair chance. I did not want him hearin' about Black startin' drama, so leaving was the best option, get me?"

"Yeah," Campbell says. "Sure."

"They ain't seen each other since, and I don't want them seeing each other tonight." I shake my head. "Bet your cousins ain't all up in your business like mine."

"No." She sounds real quiet and folds her arms and looks away. I don't like that she looks so sad, especially because Marcus's nosiness triggered it. I'll leave her alone, though. I wouldn't want anybody to put me on blast in front of a bunch of strangers. Besides, Marcus is on us like white on rice, and I have to worry about that instead.

We start heading toward Seventh Ave. I walk as many paces ahead of Marcus as I can. Campbell keeps up with me. She clearly doesn't want to walk with him. If her

probably thinking I'm not all that enthusiastic about him. "Definitely annoying too."

"See?" I smile. "I knew you get it."

And now we do laugh together, and sure enough from behind us, Marcus puts on his deep voice and calls, "Whatchy'all laughing about?"

We get back down to the same smile-laugh from before.

"Listen, Campbell Soup, I have an idea."

"Of course you do," she says, but she don't sound mad. She sounds like she wants to laugh again.

"When we get down to Seventh, you distract Marcus for me."

Her breath catches a little. "Are you sure about that?"

"Yeah, come on. I'll slip away, and then Marcus can take you home."

"I'm not sure, Lena—"

"Please," I say. If I have to beg, I will. This is that important. "I can't let him try to intimidate Black. I can't. Black wouldn't respond well to that."

I did not mean to be that honest, but her big ol' eyes are on me. She shoots me a knowing look. I hide the rest of my embarrassment in a grin. For the first time since I got a Coke thrown all over me, I feel okay with Campbell.

We walk in silence for a while. Except for my irritating cousin walking with us, I'm actually enjoying the moment. My heart is racing from the excitement of heading toward

Black. I'm so close. There's a nice breeze on my face. Could be left over adrenaline from escaping the school, but I'm amped, ready to ditch Marcus with Campbell's help, and ready to see bae.

I look up and realize there's people out everywhere. I should be glad to see that because this is normal for a Friday night. But it still seems off—because literally everybody is headed down to Seventh. All these people can't be going down to that protest—right?

We pass Ms. Johnson's house. Of course, she's standing outside on her porch, wearing leather slippers and a flowered housecoat, like always. I wave at her, but I'm shaking my head. I told her she should go to the Stein Mart that opened over in Northlake because they have real cute clothes for ladies Ms. Johnson's age. I even offered to go with her. She didn't want to. Campbell halfway lifts her hand like she's not sure if she's supposed to know this lady or not. I laugh. Obviously, she moved here recently, and not from somewhere else in the South, because she clearly doesn't get that's just the way it is here.

"Hey, Ms. Johnson," Marcus yells.

"Hey, baby, you takin' the girls home?"

"No, ma'am. My little cousin got it in her mind that she wanna go to Seventh Ave tonight."

I make a disgusted sound under my breath. "Shut up, Marcus." Campbell suppresses a giggle.

"Miss Lena James, you are not. Do I need to call Frank?"

My pulse starts to race. After all this trouble to keep tonight off Pops's radar, I'm gonna get busted by a detective in a housecoat! "It's fine, Ms. Johnson. Me and my friend meetin' someone to get a ride home. We're okay."

"Ohh, NaNa," whispers Marcus. "Lightning gonna strike you dead for lyin' to Ms. Johnson."

"She is not a preacher, you genius. Chill out."

He chuckles and calls, a little louder, "Don't worry, Ms. Johnson. I got this."

"Okay," she says, sounding pleased. "You stay with them, you hear? And y'all be careful out here, look like people acting a plum fool tonight. Look at what happened up there at that school. An officer was shot, and nineteen people was hurt in one way or another. And I reckon Seventh is only going to get worse. Heard there's already trouble brewing."

I have to admit that doesn't sound good. Ms. Johnson has the pulse of this neighborhood. She's better than Black Twitter at keeping up with news.

"I keep telling them that," Marcus says. "But they don't want to listen."

"Well, I don't advise you head that way," Ms. Johnson says. "There was a big group raising they voices about the governor. Now, that's the right thing for them to do, but it's not the right place for y'all to be."

133

Marcus probably wants to yell *I told you so*, but as I turn around and look at the smirk on his face, I can tell he's satisfied with me having heard the conversation. Sheesh. Ms. Johnson got me a little nervous, but I don't want to say so.

Campbell tenses up.

"Listen," I whisper to her. "Ms. Johnson don't do nothing but stand on her porch, tryna run this neighborhood. She has no idea what's happening down Seventh."

Campbell nods. But when she's not watching, I shoot a text to Black using Campbell's phone and also send up a quick prayer that he didn't already go home. As we walk on, I try real hard not to think about the last time he did that, when I was supposed to meet him at the studio but Wink got some last-minute tickets to a concert, and Black left and forgot to tell me.

A few houses on, I no longer believe my own words. The more I walk, the more that excitement I was feeling turns to nervousness. I recognize a few people from school, store workers, folks I've seen around. There's way too many people to make sense for this street, this time of night.

I'm really starting to wonder if Marcus and his friends weren't straight for once. This situation don't look good. But I can't turn back. Black's waiting for me.

PART III

THE FIRST BRICK

17

CAMPBELL

Seventh Avenue

We hear Seventh Avenue before we see it. Hip-hop music blares from a block away—electronic club versions of songs that play on the radio. The bass rumbles through me, not making me want to dance. Tonight, the rhythm makes me nervous.

With Marcus still playing Follow the Leader, we come to a halt at the intersection. All down the street, as far as I can see, people are partying like it's New Year's Eve, not a random Friday night in October.

My father would kill me if he knew I was down here this late. He forbid me to be on Seventh after eight o'clock. I'm not even allowed to visit his store. This street is not safe, he says. I feel it now, the nervousness in his voice when he told me to beware of this area.

That same nervousness radiates through Lena, when she says, low and soft, "Yo, Seventh is turnt."

That feels like an understatement. We're at the top of the commercial district. At this end, most of the stores are closed for the night. But one block down, people fill the sidewalks and spill over into the street. The restaurants and bars look crowded to bursting. The music competes with the sounds of the Hawks game on the bar TVs. I stare around me. There's so much going on, I wish I could open my eyes wide enough to see everything all at once. People are everywhere. Mostly black, but some white too. The men wear T-shirts and fancy sneakers. The women wear skinny jeans tucked into high-heeled boots, even if the weather is too hot for that. I see quite a few BLACK LIVES MATTER shirts and another one that's new to me—black with white block writing that says COLORED PERSON in huge letters covered by one of those red "no" symbols. I don't get it. The shirt must mean something, because there's, like, twenty-five people in those shirts, milling around. And they're holding signs made of poster board, though I can't see what's on them. As far as I can tell, all they're doing is talking to each other, but I think these must be the protestors Pee Wee and Ms. Johnson mentioned.

"Is it always like this?" I ask, aware that I sound a little awed, but not caring enough to attempt a mask of cool. Lena already thinks I'm totally naive.

"Well, Seventh usually poppin', but not like this." She's

140

still holding my phone, her nails tapping on the plastic case. I can't hear the clicks over the noise of the street, but I imagine they're staccato and anxious.

I follow her gaze toward a couple of people I can't believe I didn't notice before. A trio of white guys walks up the street, shoulder to shoulder, taking up as much of the sidewalk as they can, forcing people to step into the road to avoid them. They stand out like nothing else on this out-of-control street, wearing more camo clothing than the army and a hat with a Confederate flag on the front.

"Not like this," she says again, thoughtfully.

A crowd gathers around us, pressing closer to look at the guys across the street. Marcus and a few others start muttering.

"He better be real sure of himself, wearing that hat in this part of town."

"He better hope he bulletproof."

"Comin' down here to start trouble in our peaceful assembly."

"Don't nothin' have to stay peaceful, though. Cops all cleared outta here already."

The more they talk, the louder they get. My hands start to shake. I hide them in my pockets and edge closer to Lena and Marcus. I've never seen a street as alive as this, but it's too intense. Like an electric wire has come loose and charged every person in the crowd. I really want to get out of here.

"Where this man of yours supposed to be at?" Marcus

demands over his shoulder, his watchful eyes on the guys across the street.

"Imma call him." She puts my phone to her ear. But a couple seconds later, she lowers it again.

"He didn't answer?" Marcus shakes his head. "How often he be doin' that, NaNa? Not answering when you call?"

"He prolly can't hear over all this noise," she snaps, waving her hand in front of us.

Aw, poor girl. I don't think that's true. From what I've heard about Black tonight, he seems like the type of guy to screen his girlfriend's calls until it's convenient for him. But I can't say that. Lena looks so defeated as she turns her face back to my screen and dials again and again, waiting for an answer I don't think is going to come. I know the feeling of waiting for a call from someone you're desperately missing. Someone who's too busy in their new life to make time for what they left behind.

"It is really loud," I say. "We probably wouldn't hear a ring either. Lena, you should put the phone on vibrate, so we don't miss it when Black calls you back."

She beams at me, mouth full of blaring white teeth.

Marcus snorts and looks between us. "No idea why an epic chick like you is hollerin' at him when he whack as hell. No idea why a white girl cosignin' it."

"As I keep tellin' you, Marcus, nobody asked your opinion," Lena says.

She starts forward, heading south, wading right into the crowd. One of the two clubs on the street—dark and closed up whenever I pass during the day—is not far away and clearly open for business tonight. A pulsating line has formed outside the door, with red velvet ropes and a mountain-sized bouncer.

Lena laughs. "Girl, close that mouth or you gon' catch every mosquito on Seventh Ave in there."

My hand flies up to my mouth, which is hanging wide open. Oh, shoot. I snap it closed. Lena tosses her hair, which is no longer sleek and smooth like at the beginning of the night. Her blowout is starting to frizz up, like mine would if I released my bun.

"That's Deep Blue," she says, nodding at the club. "Ain't nothin' to get worked up about."

"You've been in there before?"

"Nah. But Black is gonna get me in soon. Once they start playing his beats, they won't care if I'm underage. When you're with the artist, they don't be sweatin' you 'bout no IDs."

"Bullshit artist, maybe," Marcus says.

Lena whirls around, nostrils flaring. Her mouth opens to snap back at him, and that's when it happens. A big, silver-gray SUV swerves toward the curb. There's a squeal of brakes, the scrape of metal on concrete and screams. People try to jump out of the way, but there's one person, a woman, who can't quite move fast enough. I think she might have been in the street, but I'm not sure. The details whiz past too fast for me to process. To realize where she was before the car hits her.

Holy crap! The car *hit her*.

She goes flying forward and crashes through a group of people in line for the club. I scream, but I can't hear myself over the chaos breaking out.

The woman's on the ground. A few people crouch down by her, and the crowd surges, pushing me forward. Those people in the protest shirts are the first ones to come running, and there are so many of them! Lena grabs onto the strap of my backpack and holds tight. I stretch and crane, trying to see what happened to the lady, but more yelling draws my attention to the street. To the car, which has rolled to a stop beside the curb. To the people who are shouting:

"What the hell?"

"Fool, where your mind at?"

"You didn't see the sista standing there?"

A few people, mostly guys, step into the street, surrounding the car. Blocking it in. Banging on the hood. Demanding the driver get out. The door cracks open and a head appears in the car door frame, and then the night explodes in front of me all over again.

"It's a damn cracker!"

"Mighta known they'd come up in here, runnin' over people like ain't no big deal."

Someone grabs the driver and hauls him from the car, flinging him into the street.

Oh, no, not again. My heads spins, and I go hot all over. I'm being pushed and shoved, caught in a wave of people. A wave that might drown me.

Hands grab me, and I gasp—it's just Lena, clutching me. She says something that gets swept away in the noise of the fight, but I can hear the tone. She's terrified, and I am too.

I glance around for her cousin. He's as transfixed by the fight as I am. The confusion has pushed us away from him. Five or six bodies separate us.

"Lena," I cry, pointing at him.

She blinks, taking a few seconds to see what's freaking me out. Her eyes get wild.

"Marcus!" she hollers. He doesn't look our way. "Marcus!"

We're getting shoved back. He's drifting away with the crowd, carried by their momentum into the street. A burst of flutters explodes inside me. He'll be gone in a second. Lena might find him annoying, but I appreciated having him around. It didn't feel quite so alone with the three of us walking together.

He's almost on the other side of the car. To get to him would mean getting in the middle of a fight. Another fight.

I am not doing that again.

18

LENA

Seventh Ave

Ms. Johnson's words come back to me about this not being the right place to be. Somehow Marcus has got himself drowned in the crowd. I can only still see him because he's so tall. I wave over my head, yelling once more, "Marcus!"

Fortunately, this time he notices. "NaNa, get out of here."

Maybe before I was trying to ditch him, but what kind of cousin would I be if he walked me all the way down here and I left him?

"Come on." I wave toward myself with both hands. He tries to fight his way out, but it ain't working.

He shouts, "Go on. Go home! Don't wait on me."

I look at Campbell. I'm kinda surprised she didn't run, but I'm grateful. My eyebrows go up. I shrug and hold my hands out, asking her what she wants to do. She frowns, looking from me to Marcus, who we can't really see anymore.

"He said to go," she says, like she's asking.

Yeah, he did. I guess we should go. With one last look at Marcus, I grab her hand and start to push my way down Seventh.

Black not answering his phone has left a pit in my stomach. The only reason I drug us all the way over to Seventh is to meet him. I can't even get ahold of him. With Marcus's words in my head, I'm having a hard time not thinking the worst. Of all nights, he has to come through for me tonight. I like a touch of drama every now and again, but this is over the top. I never wanted to star in an action thriller.

In front of me, a sea of people blocks the street I need to get across. These nosy asses are all moving toward the accident, trying to lookie-loo. And the smell on this street is rank. The people pulsing around us are all sweaty, overheated, and dirty. They funkin' up the place.

A bottle flies through the air right over me. What the hell? I barely duck in time to keep my head on. That alone scares the crap out of me. Campbell felt it too. With each unbelievable moment, we've pulled each other tighter. Despite her arm being moist from sweat, which would normally gross me out, I feel so much better holding on to her.

People are yelling at the driver. I can see his face. Aw man, homie, your timing couldn't be any worse. I almost feel sorry for him because I bet he didn't think he was gonna get dragged out his big-ass car and beat. But he did hit that lady.

The street's getting louder and louder. Those three redneck white boys that was making a scene before roll up, jumping out of a pickup truck. They park right in the middle of the street and fly into the brawl, shouting, "Get these thugs under control!"

Bodies go rushing around us. People throw punches. And aw, hell. Campbell! I have got to get her out of here. If I've learned any lessons from watching the news with Pops, it's that when situations get to this level, you never know what people might do. I don't want her to get hurt. We keep getting pushed around, trying to weave our way out of this crowd. All that has happened tonight finally drops on me, and I'm numb. My feet are moving, but nothing else.

Crack! I jump. Another bottle hits the ground nearby.

Where'd that come from? I swivel my head and see a little ways down, the patio of the Shamrock bar is bubbling. That entire strip of restaurants has really cool tables out front so people strolling by can hear the live music they got on the weekend and see what delicious treats they're serving. Now, everybody's rushing outside to see what's going on, turning that patio into an ant farm. They're making a bad situation worse. That's where all the bottles coming from—not only beer either. Someone with pretty good aim chucks a liquor bottle that smashes through the window of the SUV.

There's a flicker to my left. Somebody done lit a T-shirt on fire and threw it at the car. It goes through the smashed window, lands on the liquor and *whoosh!* The seat goes up in flames. Before I can really react to all of that, a brick smashes through a storefront window next door.

"Campbell, we gotta haul ass," I say, tugging her arm. She's mesmerized by the flames, and her feet ain't moving. "Now!"

"'Kay," she says.

We try to run, but we can't move fast. There's so many people coming this way. It's like that car crash turned all these people into zombies and they can't help but walk into the apocalypse. Why would you literally be a moth to the flames? You get hurt running toward danger—the perpetrators always walk away and the innocents get dead.

I hear a siren, but only one. Shouldn't there be more?

"Which way are we going?" Campbell shouts. "Is Black still at the tattoo parlor, do you think?"

"I don't know. Maybe. At this moment, though, we need to get somewhere safe."

"Where?" she asks.

I don't have an answer.

I search for my cousin. He's gone, swept away in the

crowd. I do see some guy climb on top of a car. Then a bunch of dudes follow him, scrambling over the hood and onto the roof. They start jumping around, caving in the roof and kicking out the windshield. A spray of broken glass showers the ground. One of the dudes tears the mirror off the side of the car like he the Hulk and throws it at another dude, smashing right at our feet.

Campbell screeches and jumps up. "That could have hit us!"

"Let's see someone try to throw something at us," I say, high-stepping over the glass. I miss the mark, because I instantly feel the sting of glass ripping across the side of my foot. I bend down and carefully try to clear out my sandal and save my skin. A beer bottle rolls toward me. I snatch it up, luckily grabbing the neck instead of the busted side. This I can use to keep the killers off us.

We finally get clear of the crowd, and I try to breathe, but the smoke from that car fire is getting heavy. I look back for a quick second because I can't help myself. Through the hazy air, a sandwich board from outside the pizza place flies by, and people hustle around, smashing windows to get inside stores.

That happened so fast.

"There!" Campbell suddenly shouts.

I follow the direction of her pointing hand, and right across the street I see one of the little convenience stores on the street, the kind that sell you a cheap hotdog with an expensive Coke.

"They closin' up. They ain't gonna let us in."

"They will. I know them. Kind of."

Shaking my head again, I let her pull me to the door. I rattle the handle, but it's locked. Story of my life tonight. But Campbell's not giving up. She's banging on the door and shouting. Gotta hand it to her, her determined side sure came out once they started burning cars. And plot twist! I'm wrong. The older man inside sees Campbell and unlocks the door.

19

CAMPBELL

Seventh Avenue

Mr. Wells opens the door to Seventh Avenue Sundries, and Lena and I tumble through, elbowing him out of the way.

"Thank you!" I set my hand on my chest and try to breathe evenly, but all I can do is pant. My pulse rate might never slow down again.

"Campbell, what are you doing here? Why are you outside in this?"

"I, um—" I look away from his face, which is drawn and wrinkled with worry and anger and maybe fear. "I didn't mean to be."

Mr. and Mrs. Wells have owned Seventh Avenue Sundries for longer than my dad's owned Carlson's. I met them when I first moved here, and he showed me around. We had lunch at the sports bar across the street, and then we stopped into their store for Tastykakes, which are sold all over up north, but down here, only the Wellses have them, I think because they're originally from Pennsylvania too. I snort when I realize that was only a couple of months ago.

The sound of shattering glass makes me jump. Another car window breaking. I sneak a peek at Mr. Wells. I don't think I've ever seen a grown-up look so scared before. He's having a full-on *the killer is inside the house* moment. He scratches his head and mumbles something I can't understand. Then, louder, he orders, "Get back. Get away from the door."

I catch sight of the metal baseball bat he's holding and the way he plants himself in front of the door like a guard. I gulp.

Lena's voice sounds from behind me, cursing. She's got my phone to her ear again. Guess her boyfriend is still not answering. I doubt she's going to hear from him again tonight. That makes him a serious jerk. I wish for a second that I was brave enough to tell Lena what I think. But we're not friends like that.

Shaking my head, I turn back to the window and slide forward, trying to see what's going on outside. Mr. Wells frowns. "Get back from the glass, young lady."

I flinch because I'm not used to being ordered around like that. Neither of my parents ever scold me. Mr. Wells's voice is firm, so I recede. But I can't stop myself from peeking at the door. I've still got a good view of the street.

There's a guy swinging an orange cone around his head like a cowboy with a lasso. Not the kind of cone the school uses in PE either. He's got one of those big traffic cones, with the black weighted bases.

"What's he going to do with that?"

Good thing I wasn't asking anyone in particular because no one responds. But not more than a minute goes by before it becomes clear what he's going to do with the cone. He torpedoes toward the cars parked across the street, hefts the cone, and smashes the windshield of the last car in the row. I gasp. The guy swings again, using the heavy base to smash another window. And another. He walks down the entire row of cars, shattering every single one.

"These punks!" Mr. Wells grumbles. "No respect for property! Who do those cars belong to, that's what I want to know!"

Out in the street, someone comes up behind the cone guy and wallops him. They start pushing and shoving. I can't tell who's on whose side. Are there sides? Mostly, this seems like a massive crowd fighting and destroying stuff. The first guy flings the cone, which smashes into some outdoor seating at Harry's Bar & Grill next door.

Instant uproar.

Tables topple. The trendy firepit in the middle of the patio falls over. Something catches, maybe a tablecloth, and with a *whoosh*, flames flicker to life.

People run, scrambling.

I can't really see what's happening, just that too many people in a too-small space are panicking, tripping, falling against the half-stone wall that barricades the patio from the street. Others jump the wall to escape the spreading fire.

A smoky haze covers the patio as it empties of people. Some head to the street, but I think some others went back inside.

God, I hope there was an emergency exit.

"What the hell?" Lena's beside me again.

"This is outrageous," I say.

I glance at the other stores and shops nearby and notice the bars are pushing people out into the street. Stores are shuttering. Two guys come out of a clothing store and start hauling one of those rolling metal doors down over the storefront. Next door, at the hookah shop my dad always hustled me past quickly, another guy yanks a security grill closed. Before he can lock it into place, two guys jump him, wrestling it open again.

"Why?" Lena groans as they throw the store worker to the ground.

One of the guys raises his foot and slams through the door, busting the glass to rush inside. Others follow.

I see why Mr. Wells is guarding his door with a baseball bat. He knew. He knew what was coming. He knew the looting would start. A flash of heat blazes in my head, sparking trickles of sweat at my temples.

"I can't take any more," I whisper. What if we were still out there? What if Mr. Wells hadn't opened the door and let us in? We'd be in the middle of that. Tears prick my eyes.

Then, I catch sight of the strangest episode yet. Huge sheets of plywood go marching toward the window. A whole stack. The person carrying it staggers under the weight. Mr. Wells bounds forward and opens the door to admit the plywood. As he helps lower the load, I see who's carrying the load.

Nicky, the weekend manager of my father's hardware store down the road.

Nicky, who is supposed to be in charge of the store this weekend while my father fishes at his cabin.

Nicky, who is not minding the store right now at all.

"I got as much as I could carry," he says, leaning the wood against the door frame. He pulls two hammers and a box of nails from his apron pocket. The apron that is his uniform when he's working at my dad's store. "It might not be enough, but we'll make do. No way can I get back down the street with all—"

"What are you doing here?" I demand.

He turns to me, and his eyes go wide. "What are you doing here?"

"Who's this?" Lena asks.

"My dad's manager!" I say at the same time Mr. Wells says, "My grandson."

"You're supposed to be at the store!" I'm yelling. Loud enough that Lena startles and stares at me.

"I locked the door!"

His defensive tone adds the context. We both know that doesn't matter. A lock? A second ago, I watched a guy kick down a security door. A lock isn't going to stop anyone from getting into my dad's shop!

"I set the alarm too," Nicky says.

Lena snorts. "Look around. They rioting. You think the po po gon' show up for an alarm at one little store? Naw, man. Whenever they do get around to getting here, they gon' be too busy tear gassin' folks to worry about some hammers and nails at the hardware store."

A sob catches in my throat. She's right. The store is totally unprotected. My dad is screwed. And I am too.

"Look, it happened fast. I…I didn't know what to do. I'm sorry. But it's done now." Nicky sets about trying to drag the plywood all the way into the convenience store. I step forward, blocking him.

"Move," he says.

I flinch, but I don't give up any ground. "You have to go back. You have to go back to my dad's store this minute!"

"What? Do you see what's happening out there?"

"Do *you*?" I start pushing the plywood back out the door. "This belongs to my father. Did you pay for it?"

He has the sense to look a little ashamed, but growls, "Are you accusing me of stealing?"

Mr. Wells, who's been standing there dumbfounded, comes back to life. "Of course we will pay for this. Of course we will. This is an emergency. My grandson must help us board up the windows. They could throw bricks any minute."

Nicky glares at me. I glare back. He retaliates by giving the sheets of wood a huge shove. I lose my grip and stumble back. My butt hits the ground.

"Yo," Lena says, stepping in front of me. The face she turns on Nicky is hard, and she's got a broken bottle clutched in her hand. "Back up."

Nicky jumps, shouting, "What the heck?!"

Mr. Wells rushes in, grabbing his grandson. "Get out, get out! You're not going to rob me!"

"Oh, I'm a thief?" Lena shouts. "Y'all got a lotta nerve sayin' that, when this boy admitted to stealing her dad's wood."

"That's not what happened!" Mr. Wells brandishes his bat. "Who do you think you are, saying that?"

I duck and throw my hands over my head. Is he really going to hit us? This is ludicrous. Lena does not look intimidated by him or the bat.

"Your worst nightmare, if your grandson puts his thieving hands on her again."

I gasp. She's been surprising me all night, but this is different. Lena might have the biggest balls of anyone I have ever met. Maybe Mr. Wells thinks so too, because he stops. His chest rises and falls too fast, and he's dripping sweat at his temples. After a long, terrible stare down between him and Lena, Mr. Wells lowers the bat and holds out his other hand, palm up.

"Okay, enough," he says. His voice trembles. "We will not bring the fight in here."

I look from him to Lena. I can only see her profile, the muscle jumping in her jaw, and I find myself silently begging both of them to take a deep breath. Lena loosens her grip on the bottle and lowers it to her side. She reaches down to help me up, while Nicky, a triumphant smile on his face, pushes the boards inside and locks the door. Tears trickle from my eyes. I've lost.

"Does my dad know?" I sound whiny and pathetic in my own head, and I cast my eyes downward so I can't see the others' reactions.

"Yes! I mean, I left him a message. Once he hears—"

"There's no reception at his cabin." I'm crying in earnest. Lena puts an arm around me.

"Here is what we must do," Mr. Wells says. "We will board up these windows. Campbell, you go in the back and wait there. And this girl—"

Lena bristles, and I jump in, "My friend. Lena."

"Well. Then you both wait in the back. Mr. Carlson would want me to look out for you. When Nicky is finished, he will take you home."

I look from Nicky's smug face to the chaotic street beyond the window. Someone flies past holding an armload of clothing I'm sure they didn't pay for. My father's store is all we have. What's going to happen to us—to me—if everything gets stolen tonight? I can't let that happen. Mr. Wells is standing here with his grim look, ready to defend his store with a *baseball bat*. I can't go home. I have to do something.

"I'm going to my dad's store."

Everyone hollers at once.

Lena's protective arm becomes a barricade. "What the hell are you talking about? You finna get yo-self hurt! We ain't goin' out there."

"You don't have to come."

Her face twists. "You goin' by yourself? Really?"

"Don't be ludicrous, Campbell," Nicky says. He's already begun nailing his contraband plywood to the inside of the store windows. "You can't go protect your father's store."

"Well, if you had stayed where you were supposed to, I wouldn't have to!"

"Campbell Soup," Lena says. "Come on. Think for a minute. It ain't safe. If we wait until I—"

"Until what? Black calls back? You're all about him,

aren't you? Well, I'm not! And I can't wait around for him while my family loses all we have!"

She looks like I slapped her. I'm sorry for that. I shouldn't yell, and this isn't really about her, but I'm freaking out.

"Girls, I cannot let you consider this," Mr. Wells begins, but Lena cuts him off with a death glare.

"Who you tryna tell what to do?" She flips her hair over her shoulder and turns her back on him. "We have to hook up with Black and his boys. The tattoo place is on the way to your dad's shop. Listen," she says, when she sees I'm about to object. "We'll be safer with them. You're gonna need help once we get down by your dad's store anyway. What if they already looting?"

My heart drops. I hadn't thought of that, but of course, she's right. I need help.

"Okay," I say. "We can try to meet up with Black—but promise me, Lena. Promise me we're really heading to my dad's store."

She nods solemnly. "You got my word."

Mr. Wells gives a sharp shake of his head. "It's not safe for you to—"

"Grandpa!" Nicky shouts. "The door!"

We all spin and see a figure hulking up behind the glass, brick in hand. He's got on a hat, and the brim shades his face, but he's white and he looks really young. Like, our age. Maybe younger. With a yell that makes me jump, Mr. Wells goes blasting out the door, swinging his bat. God, who would've thought Mr. Wells with his sweater vests and his polite, precise demeanor had such a feral creature in him?

I want to see what Mr. Wells is doing to the guy. The kid. He's just a kid, I can't believe Mr. Wells would hurt him. Then again, the kid had a brick he was about the smash through the door.

But I can't wait for this to play out. I have to get to the store. While the Wellses are distracted, I squeeze past them and out the door.

PART IV

FATAL FUNNEL

20

LENA

South on Seventh Ave

Campbell got her wings on again, and I gotta hurry. Normally, on a Friday night, this street is buzzing with people having a good time, eating, laughing, drinking. Right now, all I can see is smoke, things being thrown everywhere, from cones to chairs to protest signs, and blood on bruised bodies. As I run after Campbell, I can't stop thinking: What am I doing? I am a mess-free zone—why am I chasing this white girl out into a riot? This is wild! And all these people are headed the same way right behind us.

But Campbell been goin' hard for me tonight, so Imma ride with her.

We head down Seventh, not speaking, and that gives me a minute to think about the fact that Black didn't answer. *Again.* He can't miss what's going on outside. He down here too, ain't he? He better be at that tattoo parlor when I get there, and he better not have got himself hurt, or I'll kill him myself.

I have to get my head out of that place. I glance back. Nicky is losing a battle with someone for that plywood. It gets ripped right out his hands, and I feel what's coming next. I whip my eyes front because I don't really want to see him get his head busted.

We only make one more block before someone shoves me—and oh no. A fistfight, practically right on top of us. Campbell screams. This old man's gettin' beat up, and he's yelling for help. The other guy grabs him and swings him into a wall. I pause and eye the guy on the ground.

"I think I've been in his store before," I say. "He always yellin' at his customers. He ain't nice. He probably cussed this dude out at some point, now this dude gettin' him back." I smirk. That store owner got a nasty attitude. People only go in his shop if they don't feel like going to the mall. It's the only spot in the neighborhood that got outfits worth getting.

Campbell looks annoyed by my comment. "That's no reason to beat someone up. What if that was my father?"

"Wow, all you've seen tonight, and this is what got you mad?"

I been in her hardware store once or twice, but I can't remember if her daddy nice to his customers or not.

I shrug. My eyes follow the guy as he climbs through a broken window. He comes out the front with an armful of shirts and jeans. Then, a bright light is beaming down on us from above. I squint up into the sky and—of course, a dirty bird. I don't know who's running it—could be the po po, but might also be the news, which tend to show up when people start beating on each other. The light follows a pair of looters, switches over to some folks fighting, takes in all the other activity.

I shield my eyes with my hand, trying to see what we're dealing with here. I catch the Channel 2 logo on the side. Pops watches the news and makes me watch with him non-stop, so I know that logo well. I almost think that's worse than the cops. As Pops says, the nice folk in the suburbs like to stay good and scared of what's happening down here in the hood, so that's the story reporters always want to tell.

A voice booms from the sky, and I notice another helicopter shows up—this one with the megaphone has got to be a cop chopper. That's a sign this is truly going downhill, when everyone's in the air. One thing I'm sure of is that once the dirty birds starts swarming, people are going to jail.

Flyin' fists, blood, broken glass, burning cars, there's so much going on around us. Everywhere we look. I'm starting to be scared we ain't escaping unless it's in the back of a squad car. Which, I guess, is better than the back of an ambulance, but Pops would kill me dead if the only place he sees me tonight is on the evening news. We have got to get off the street.

We're getting shoved forward again. Two men—one darker skinned and one who looks like he might be Latino—thrust past us, huddling around a pregnant lady. I don't think they mean to hurt us; they just real focused. Bet they're trying to get her to her car. They smart. This ain't no place for a pregnant lady. But she can't move real fast because her belly is huge, and they're all awkward, trying to get away. As they knock into us, the lady drops her purse.

"Wait!" she calls. "My pocketbook! My ID, my keys!"

I kinda want to keep moving. That lady ain't my problem. But she sounds so desperate. I let go of Campbell's arm, grab the purse from the ground, and chase after them. I get close enough to reach, and then I tap her on the shoulder. Man, the shriek she lets out and the look in her eyes. You would have thought I shot her. The Latino guy reacts real fast, putting out a hand to push me away. I'm lucky he don't hit me.

I hold up the purse. "Here."

"Thank you," she gasps.

The Latino guy grabs the bag from me and yells, "Come on. We gotta go!"

And they right. I have to go too. I spin around to grab Campbell, but I can't see her. Aw, hell, where is she?

"Campbell!" I scream.

I run back to where she was when I last saw her. My mind goes blank. Feet slapping the pavement, jewelry ringing, sweat forming on my forehead. Why did I let her go? Why didn't she follow me? If I find out tomorrow something happened to her, I'm going to be sick. I finally stop and spin around on the spot. Tears form in my eyes. There ain't no mousey teenage girls anywhere in my line of sight. Have I lost her?

No, wait—there's a white girl up ahead. A little bit of hair yanked up in a bun and a face peeking out of the doorway set back from the street, but that's her, I'm pretty sure.

"Campbell!" My voice don't crack through all the noise, and she ain't lookin' in my direction. She hiding, which is smart, but we ain't gonna catch each other that way. I push and elbow my way through the people between us until I reach that doorway where I saw her. Soon as I get there, I grab her. She shrieks and tries to pull free.

"It's me, girl," I say.

She looks me in the face, and then her body relaxes. I don't. I take her shoulders and shake her. "Why didn't you stay with me?"

"Why didn't *I* stay? Why didn't you? I thought you left me." She's got tears in her eyes.

"Why would I do that?"

"Everyone does," she sobs.

171

"You still on this planet?" I realize I'm screaming, but why? I'm not mad. I can't explain how I'm feeling, but it's taking me over. "Listen, I didn't run off. We only gon' get through together."

"Okay." She wipes her eyes and links her arm through mine. "Don't let go again."

Feels like the tattoo shop where Black suppose to be at is so far away. Seventh Ave ain't that big, but we been out here so long. Time keeps ticking, and the muscles in my legs burn. My feet throb, and my shirt is soaked like I got pushed in a pool. My hair sticks to the back of my neck, so I toss it into a bun. I don't got no rubber band, but I do my best to make a knot that will stay. We have to keep going to get out of here, but I just want to sit down. I want this to be over. We bust our way through people running around, fighting each other, and destroying property. The street's so hazy, with fires poppin' up left and right, it looks out of focus. My throat is scratchy and water streams from my eyes. Beside me, Campbell pulls her T-shirt up over her mouth and nose, coughing up a lung.

The tattoo shop is up ahead, and I don't see that many people around. That's good. Yes, finally! I speed up, and Campbell follows. My heart starts to race. I'm almost at a jog. I don't bother hiding the smile on my face. Black!

I stop in front of the shop and—

"It's closed."

"No!" I scream. My knees give out, and I drop to the ground.

The light on the sign flashes an annoying OPEN in neon red letters, but the door is boarded up with fresh plywood. They slapped a BLACK-OWNED BUSINESS sign in the front, written fast and barely readable, and no one's bothered the door. But Black is definitely not here. My smile fades.

I sob, "He left!"

Why didn't he call Campbell's phone? My legs are too weak to stand back up. I'm so done. Why would he leave me, with no sign, no call, no nothing? How could he do this? I don't get it. What am I gonna do? I'm done pretending like this night is going to be okay. It's not okay, and it keeps getting worse.

"Lena." Campbell kneels next to me. She pulls me in closer to the door of the shop and puts her arm around me. I lean into her hug. I'm stuck, can't move.

"Guys are a waste," she says. "Don't let him make you cry."

"I ain't cryin'." I wipe my eyes. "I'm mad."

Campbell starts rustling through her bag and comes up with a pretty, purple water bottle with some cool metallic designs on the side. She offers me some, and I shake my head. "Girl," I say, smirking, "you just remembered you have water?"

"I've been kinda busy tonight, as it turns out."

We laugh at that, and I take a long drink, holding it up over my head so my lips don't touch. Campbell takes the bottle back, takes a sip, and then pours some into her hands. She wipes her whole face and then sticks the empty bottle back in her bag.

I look down at the screen of her phone, which is still in my hand, at all the unanswered calls I made to Black. He told me to come here, and now he not answering the phone?

"I'm callin' his ass again, and he better pick up."

She makes a face. "Are you sure?"

"Yeah, one more time, then I'm done."

LaShunda would be going ham about how Black ain't nothin' and how I got us all the way down here for nothin'. For the first time tonight, I'm glad it's Campbell I'm with, not LaShunda. I do kinda wish I could call her, just to be sure she's sitting still at home. She'll be the first person I call as soon as my phone charges. I bet she been trying to call me and getting my voicemail. Prolly worried as hell. This night has been hard on everyone.

The phone rings and rings, and then:

"Girl, where you at?"

"Where am I? At the tattoo shop where you were supposed to be," I shout. "Where are you?"

"Wait, you're at the shop?" Black says. "Why the hell'd you come down to Seventh? You shoulda gone home. Didn't you see what was happening?"

"Not 'til I got here."

"Okay, keep coming. I'm headin' to Walmart now. But you gotta hurry. People sayin' cops is turnin' up, and they got riot gear on."

"Black, can't you come get me?"

"Are you scared, baby?"

If only he knew what I been through tonight. Something crashes nearby, making me and Campbell both jump and push back farther into the doorway. Glad she thought to tuck us in here. "Yes, I'm scared. You see what's happening. But you left me and wouldn't answer your phone! Got me out here looking crazy."

"My phone died. I was charging it at the shop, then Big Baby ran in, talking 'bout it was a riot up the street. Soon as he said that, they was like, get out, we closin', and they kicked everybody out. You know how Wink is, he had to see for himself. Big Baby out there tryna keep him from being reckless. We gonna meet back at my car by the Walmart."

"Multiply that by five and that's been my night. Someone got shot up at the school, homeless dude tried to kill us, and then we was in that riot you talkin' about."

A louder crash makes me look up. A couple of guys about my cousin's age, with faces full of rage, swing chairs they must've taken from a patio, at those newspaper racks. They bolted down, so I don't get the point. One of the racks starts tilting over, and two guys kick 'til it dents in. Another guy takes a huge whack at the last rack standing, knocking off the bolts and—of course, it comes flying toward us.

"Watch out!"

Campbell shouts too, but she kicks out a leg real quick and knocks the rack out of the way.

"Go, Campbell!" I say, then stop when I realize she's whimpering and holding her ankle. "Campbell Soup, you okay?"

She nods and pushes her foot down. "It's okay. I think it's maybe just bruised. I can walk."

"What's goin' on?" Black's yelling into the phone.

"We under attack out here!"

"Tell me you safe, baby, tell me you okay."

"I'm not hurt, but I ain't okay, Black!"

"I can hear it, queen. It's my turn to hold you down."

God, please, yes. Finally. I'm exhausted. Someone else can be in charge for a minute so I can rest. I'm not the type that needs a knight in shining armor, but if Black wants to ride up on a white horse, I'm getting on.

"Just need you to get to me," he says.

Get to him? I sink. My hands bang against the wall. No more.

A heavyset guy comes running out of the store next to us with an armload of snacks. A strip of lotto tickets flutters down on me. He loaded his pockets with 'em too. Campbell picks up the string of tickets from my lap, eyes all big like she can't believe what she's seeing. She flings them away from her like a dead mouse. When he goes to move on, he trips over one of them busted newspaper racks and hits the ground. Ha! That's what his thieving behind gets! I turn to Campbell whose mouth is trapped between a laugh and a frown. "Black is down the street. Let's go."

Campbell doesn't look relieved. She look mad. "No. No way. I have to check on my dad's store."

"We can't waste time on that. Black said riot police comin'."

"Lena, you promised!"

I guess I did. I scootch to the edge of the step and lean around the door frame, looking south, toward her dad's place. Whoa. Plumes of black smoke billow out across the street, so thick it looks like a solid wall.

"What is that? What's down there?"

She hacks, burying her nose on my shoulder, choking. "What?"

"Tires," she says, her voice scratchy.

Oh, right. Down the next corner is that mechanic shop Pops used to take his car to, back when he was still allowed to drive. They always had a mountain of old tires piled in back of the lot. Man, if they set those to burning, this whole place is probably about to melt down.

"Campbell," I say. "Put your wings back on."

21

CAMPBELL

Carlson's Hardware Store

We're running again. Adrenaline courses through my legs, making them tremble, but I hold back. If I run flat out, I'll lose Lena. When I turned around earlier and couldn't see her face anywhere in crowd, I almost fainted. That was the worst moment of my life. I could be at the store already if I let go and fly, but we shouldn't separate. Besides, my ankle twinges every time I step, and I'm not sure it's as okay as I thought. Maybe I couldn't fly right now, even if I wanted to.

Sweat pours off my face. My backpack bangs hollowly against my side, lighter with all the water gone. I wish we hadn't emptied it completely. My throat aches from the smoke, and the burned stench clogs my nostrils. God, what if this fire spreads down to the store? What would be worse—finding out it's been robbed or burned to ashes?

A nasty pit forms in my stomach. When my dad quit paying child support a few years ago, my mom lost her house. What will happen if the store goes? Would he go bankrupt? I'm not sure I really know what that means, but I'm guessing he'd lose everything. Where would we go? Maybe he would get an apartment. Or his fishing cabin—does he own that? Would he want me to stay with him or would my mom have to take me? If the idea of transferring me to a foreign school before the year started made her melt down, imagine asking her to move me in the middle of the year. She'd hit the roof. And so would I.

I speed up. We can't lose the store. We just…can't.

Next to my dad's store is a pharmacy, and one before that is the little organic sandwich shop where my dad was hoping I'd get a job. My stomach swoops. We're close!

The sandwich place should be closed at this time of night, but the lights are on. A group of crying girls crowds around, all dressed up like they were at one of the clubs, limping around on bare feet, high heels in their hands. The owners—a young couple my dad told me quit their corporate lawyer jobs to open the shop—appear in the doorway, huddled together. After a second, the man flips the lock, pulls his apron up over his nose and mouth, cracks open the door enough to slide outside. He steps behind the girls, a fountain of dreadlocks pulled up on top of his head, bobbing around, and begins to shoo them in. As the girls squeeze through the miniscule opening, he raises his arms protectively, swiveling his head back and forth between the street and the door. His wife, still visible in the door frame, holds a gun. Jeez.

Before I see whether he gets all the girls safely inside, we're past his place and racing by the pharmacy, which looks hard hit. All the windows and the sliding doors are shattered. A steady stream of people stumbles over broken glass to get in and out.

My dad's place is next. I run past the alley between the pharmacy and his store, glancing briefly into it. Normally, my dad parks his truck there, but of course, he's at the cabin. His truck isn't there. A faded-blue sedan sits in that spot instead, and all I can think is how annoyed my dad gets when someone takes his space. If he were here, he'd have that old beater towed in a hot minute.

And then, I hear the burglar alarm yelping futilely.

I skid to a stop in front of our door and gasp.

"No," I whisper. My shoulders begin heaving.

It's…it's destroyed. The store is demolished.

The big glass window is shattered. There was a Halloween display I helped my dad create—some pumpkins and hay bales and a homemade scarecrow on a bench wearing a button-down shirt and a store apron. The pumpkins lay on the ground, some inside and some outside, all but one smashed to sticky, slippery bits. The scarecrow's tumbled from the bench and rests pathetically on its back, straw pant legs straight up in the air. One of the hay bales is gone, flung into the street and torn open. Straw litters the display and trails out onto the sidewalk.

And the stack of the supplies we used to create the display—drills, hammers and boxes of nails, twine balls—all gone.

"OMG," Lena says.

I stare at the destruction. The door hangs from the hinges, a huge splintery crack in the center, where someone must have kicked it in. A piece breaks off, thumping my shoulder as it falls. I was too stunned see it coming. I cry out, but not from the pain. I'm so numb, I can barely feel.

"What are you doing?" Lena grabs my shirt and pulls me back. "You can't go in there! What if they still inside?"

I yank away. I have to see.

"Dear God," she whispers and scrambles after me.

The lights are all on because selfish Nicky didn't bother to turn them off before he fled, so the place doesn't feel scary. But I'm crying so hard, everything looks blurry.

They ransacked the counter, strewed papers all over, bashed open the cash register. I don't need to go over to see it's empty. As empty as the shelves. They've torn down all the merchandise, pulled products from the hooks hanging on the walls. Packaging and trash litter the floor. An end cap of batteries has been knocked over. Most are gone, but there's a few still scattered around.

I step forward and hear the snap of plastic. Under my heel is a vanity license plate, the kind you hang on a kid's bedroom door. The bright orange plastic reads DANIEL. Now, it's cracked in two. The round wire display rack that used to stand by the register lays on its side, a rainbow of vanity plates spilling across the floor.

I slide over to the next aisle.

Someone's yanked out all the boxes of nails, all those neat, orderly, carefully divided little boxes have been flung open and spilled on the floor. They didn't even take the nails. They just wrecked whatever they could get their hands on.

There's a thunk, the clank of metal on the tile floor, and the sound of voices. Lena swears under her breath. I jump, slipping a little on all the debris.

"Campbell, no," Lena whispers.

She must think I'm going to head toward the noise. Am I? I don't know what I'm going to do, but they must have heard her because suddenly, feet are thundering toward us.

Lena and I both cry out and scramble backward. Two guys burst out of the paint aisle. They're wearing hoodies pulled over their heads. One guy has a bunch of shovels. The other cradles a load of spray paint cans in the pouch of his sweatshirt. A few slip out as he passes, hitting the ground with a clunk.

Suddenly, I. Am. Pissed. An angry wave swells, rising from my feet into my head, crashing through me.

"Hey!" I lunge forward. "Get the hell out of here!"

They're running. Lena's pulling on me, hollering, "Shut up, shut up!"

"Drop that," I shout.

The guys glance at me, kick an empty box in my direction, and jump out the broken window. I follow them into the display, but they're gone. Fleeing into the crowd of other jerks who've taken merchandise they didn't pay for. Jerks who've robbed people like me and my dad out of business.

"They had no right," I cry. "No right!"

I pick up the nearest, heavy thing I can reach—a pumpkin—and heave as hard as I can. The gourd smashes against the wall, leaving a sticky orange residue behind.

"Campbell, stop," Lena says.

"Stop? Stop? Is that all you can say? Look around!"

She does, but I don't follow her gaze to the empty shelves. I can't look. All I want to do is cover my eyes. So I do, pressing my fingers down hard enough to stem the tears. I'm having trouble breathing.

"It's all gone," I gasp.

22

LENA

Carlson's Hardware Store

I've never seen any place this tore up in my life. Man, I'd hate to be on the clean-up crew that has to deal with this.

For a while, we're quiet. I walk around, looking, shuffling carefully around the nails strewn on the floor and scout around. The candy rack—the only thing I really remember from stopping in here with Pops—is mostly empty. Except for those peanut-shaped marshmallow candies that look like cardboard and make you feel like you got a mouth full of Elmer's. Of course they left those. I snicker, but then shut up when I notice Campbell sobbing on the bench in the window display.

She's pressing on her eyes. If she don't stop, she might pop 'em out.

"Hey, Campbell. You gonna be all right. That's what insurance is for, right? You can rebuild. You know what, this might be what y'all needed. The insurance money will come through, and you make your store better." Far as I can tell, people only come here when they don't got transportation to a real store like Ace. Pops always says this place is too small and too expensive. "Or your daddy could open a cool place like a hookah bar."

"What do you know?" she snaps. "That doesn't make sense."

That's rude. I was trying to help, offer her some words of encouragement, but she's all in her feelings. She pulls her hands away from her eyes, and she's full-on crying. Like sobbing. I hope she gets this out of her system soon, because we really have to go. Outside the window, smoke keeps rolling down the street and people are moving like blurs, throwing bricks and trash cans, pushing shopping carts loaded with home goods. The fire across the street pops, and the sound of cracking glass is on a loop. A female reporter holding a Chanel 5 mic, with a finger to her ear, stands on the sidewalk with her cameraman beside her, trying to report the news. She's talking to a bunch of people, and a couple of 'em got their shirts pulled up over their noses. Behind them, some dude doing circus tricks with a shopping cart, clout-chasing. I want to laugh so freaking bad, but this ain't the time. The reporter don't even realize she got a whole show happening right behind her. She looks crazy to me—reminds me of that meme of the little dog sitting in the burning house saying, "This is fine." Lady, it is not fine. Right then, a guy comes and pulls the camera out of the cameraman's hands and chucks it into the street.

We gotta get back on track.

"We have to go," I say. "This is a done deal."

"Go where? There's no place to go."

"Home, Campbell. You can go home. Look, we saw what's out there. Helicopters, looters, this has turned into the Wild West. Won't be much longer before they start lockin' down the streets, and then we'll be trapped. We could get arrested. Or shot. We running out of luck, for real."

I pause, hoping my little pep talk is enough to get her going. This right here is about getting out.

"I can't abandon my dad's store."

"Abandon what? Look around you, fool. There ain't nothin' here left to protect!"

"You're right." She sobs harder. "We have nothing left."

"This can all be replaced. Can't replace us if someone comes in here and cracks our head open because they want a power tool or a hammer. Or if the cops run up in here and want to put my ass in jail because they think I'm the one takin' things."

"You don't get it," she says, tears running down her face. "This place is all my dad has."

"I don't understand? You got us sitting in a broken

window like ducks at a carnival game lined up to get popped. Quit crying over a store! You so busy feeling sorry for yourself, we gonna get killed."

"Stop screaming at me."

"Stop whining like a two-year-old. Get your ass up."

"Why are you so angry?"

This girl got some nerve. Like she's the only person who had a rough night. "You haven't seen me angry yet."

"You know what, Lena? Go. Your only concern is getting to your worthless boyfriend, who clearly doesn't even care if you're safe or not, considering he's ditched you twice already!"

I. See. Red. "For the record, he did not ditch me. He was waiting for me."

"Whatever."

I spin toward the broken window. "I'm not dying with you tonight."

23

CAMPBELL

Carlson's Hardware Store

Lena hops over the jagged glass left in the window frame and lands on the sidewalk outside. Her fury still boils in the air after she's gone.

She just doesn't get it. If she would get her head out of that guy's butt, she would see he's not the superhero she thinks he is.

But alone in the display area, with no window glass to dampen the sound, the roar of shouting and the crackling of the fire grow loud in my ears. My eyes sting from the smoke, and a heaviness settles on me. I kick at one of the remaining pumpkin shards, feeling scolded. My shoulders are weights, dragging me into a slump. My fingertips weigh a hundred pounds each, pinning my hands uselessly to the bench.

I hate everything. This washed-up store. My father, for

being broke. My mother, for taking a job in Venezuela. This city and these fucked-up people for rioting. I mean, rioting! How the hell does tearing down my father's store help?

And Lena. Stuck-up, snobby Lena and her loser boyfriend who is never going to love her like she wants. Lena, who left me for him anyway.

A plume of black smoke drifts through the window, sending me into a hacking fit. I lift the collar of my shirt, wiping my face, my tears, my sweat, my snot. When I let the shirt flop back into place, it's wet and sticky against my skin. Ewww. A yell goes up outside. I close my eyes. I should probably check out what that is. Or get back inside the store and hide. Or take some action other than sit here, but I can't. When I open my eyes, the wreckage of my life will still be there, scattered on the floor among the shards of pumpkin and broken glass.

Actually, what I really want to do is turn over the reins of this whole terrifying, shambles of a night to a grown-up. Time to call my dad. I pat my pocket, and—oh, crap! Lena has my phone. I'm on my feet, jumping out the window, though I'll probably never catch up with her. She's probably halfway to that guy already, halfway home—

She's right outside. Hasn't gone ten feet. Before I stop to consider why that might be, I reach around and snatch my phone from her hand.

"I'll take that back, if you don't mind!"

She doesn't object, which surprises me, because that phone has been her life support all night. She's frozen, and as my brain catches up to my motion, I process the almost-hush that's fallen. I peek over Lena's shoulder.

Whoa.

A few blocks down, a human wall stretches across the street. Police officers, dressed in black, wearing helmets, standing four or five deep. Maybe more. They stretch so far back, I can't count them. Somewhere at the back, I see— Jesus. Horses?

The front line stands shoulder to shoulder, holding clear shields nearly as tall as their bodies, emblazoned with the word POLICE. The light from the streetlamps glints off the plastic. Each officer holds a long wooden stick that looks like a human-size baton. My breath catches.

Little noises pierce the quiet—one or two shouts, the crackle of flames—but that's all. Fire streaks along the road here and there. The wind shifts, blowing a cloud of smoke through and over the line of cops, turning them into indistinct silhouettes—like robot soldiers in a sci-fi movie.

I close my eyes. I don't want to see this. It's not happening. I'm not here.

I wish I were at home. In my old house, in my old neighborhood, with my old friends, where I didn't know what gunshots sound like in real life or how fire looks reflecting off riot gear.

I wish I were back at school, hiding in Ms. Marino's classroom.

Lena's warnings about ending up dead don't feel like drama anymore. Ending up dead feels…possible.

Even with my eyes closed, I can't imagine myself away from here. The horses' hooves clip-clop on asphalt as they shift around, and I hear that. Broken glass crunches beneath boots, and I hear that. A thousand chests heave and breathe heavily, and I hear all of them. Even with my eyes closed, I know exactly where I am.

A shout pierces the near hush. My legs start to shake. A roar of voices explodes. I snap open my eyes in time to see a trash can full of fire go flying through the air. Toward the police.

Oh God.

I scream. Lena does too, and we grab each other, pressing back into the shattered glass window display of my dad's store. My arm scrapes the edge. Blood begins to ooze.

The trash can hits the ground with a thud—nowhere near the cops—but that doesn't matter. I'm too afraid to poke my head out and look down the street, but I don't need to. Boots start hitting the asphalt—dozens. Hundreds. Marching forward. Pounding rhythmlessly.

The crowd surges too. Those protestors in their matching shirts hurtle toward the police, and I want to yell at them to stop. They're going to get hurt! Can't they see how dangerous this has gotten? But they don't look afraid. Every single face rushing past looks hard and determined.

No. Not every face. People are fleeing too—screaming and crying, running, falling, getting trampled.

My arm throbs. My heart pounds. My heads spins like I might faint.

"What do we do?" I shout, looking at Lena.

One look at her face tells me she's as frightened as I am, and she has no more idea what to do than me. She looks exactly like she looked when she saw the lights and sirens at school. Out on the street, the line of cops crashes into the line of rioters and protestors, shields smashing into bodies, knocking them down, sticks crashing on heads. A few people swing broken street signs at the shields, cracking them.

Lena screams again.

24

LENA

Seventh Ave

I'm gonna get hurt if I don't come up with a plan to get myself out of here. I been the answer queen all night, but I'm out of ideas. Maybe I used up every one I had in my head.

"We have to run."

There it is, my million-dollar plan. Run.

We lock eyes. I give Campbell a nod, and we start battling our way through. Seventh Ave looks like a war zone. Not too long ago, before we came into the hardware store, I could still sorta see cars, that pile of burning tires, people. The smoke has taken over. There's black at the edges of my vision, and all I can see is one tunnel right in front of me. My chest is tight, tears are forming in my eyes.

I grab Campbell's hand tighter, because our palms are so sweaty, we're slipping out of each other's grip. I can't do that. She would be lost if I did that. I'd be lost.

"Keep to the edges," Campbell shouts.

We try to, but people are running everywhere, getting knocked over. Someone bumps us, and we fall on the pile of people. I land on my back. My elbow drags along the pavement, skin ripping open and collecting gravel. I'm hollering, scrambling backward on my butt like some kinda crab trying to get away, but my shoe pops. The leather breaks, and now I just have a sole.

Campbell grabs me. "Come on. In a few blocks, we can get off Seventh—I think I remember where to turn." She takes off, pulling me behind her. Campbell's voice snaps me back into this universe, and I keep replaying one word in my mind: *run*.

I'm so focused on the direction I'm running—it's like I'm wearing blinders like the horses in those races Pops like to watch—I almost miss him. I almost miss Black.

Oh, my God, Black!

"Queen!" He catches hold of me, grabs me to keep me from running past him. The tears I've been trying so hard to hold back begin to flow. I mean, dear God, finally, finally! My knees buckle, and I fold. My hair falls over my face, and hopefully my tears.

"I can't believe we found each other," I say. "It's a miracle."

"Lena?" Campbell's shaky voice strains to get heard over the noise.

I forgot she was even here. My body had dumped out all

196

that was weighing me down at one time. When I'm done, I stand up, face to face with Black, who's staring at me.

"You okay?"

I collapse in his arms.

"I got you," he says. "Let's get outta here."

I nod. "Come on, Campbell."

"If we go another couple minutes down that way," she says, pointing toward the south, "we can get off this street."

"Black!" Peanut yells. I look past Black and see all the usual suspects, Peanut's skinny tail always jumping around like he's an extra from a music video, Wink, scanning the street watching what's happening, and Big Baby, big silly grin, as usual.

"A'ight, man," Black says. "We comin'!"

"We?" Peanut looks from Black to me to Campbell and starts waggin' his head. "That's on you."

Black shrugs. "Who requested different?"

"Why we goin' south?" Big Baby says. "Peanut, your car closer."

Wink cuts him off with a shove. "Are you serious? Shut up."

"If Peanut's car is closer, then that's where we need to go," Black says.

"Whatever, Black, don't be feeling yourself around shorty," Peanut says.

I shake my head. These boys aren't good at keeping

themselves organized, so I always have to do it for them. "Y'all, we really need to keep goin'," I say, being the voice of reason. "A lot is coming our way."

We maneuver to the outside of the crowd with Wink in the lead. Peanut walks almost in step with Wink, then Big Baby, then Black, keeping me and Campbell tucked between him and the buildings to our left. I try to keep pace with everybody even though my broken shoe flaps against my ankle and slows me down. Black has his arm around me and that feels amazing, and I'm focused on that. The soft fabric of his jacket cuff brushes my neck. Somehow this makes me feel good. With each swipe, I'm reminded that he's right there with me. And Campbell, she sticks close too. We're still holding hands.

Even with the relief of the moment, I can't help but notice these fools look kinda roughed up. Peanut is bleeding from a cut on his face. Big Baby eyes streaming and his T-shirt is ripped. They clearly been through some craziness tonight too. My heart jumps. Black might not have come through for me earlier when I first needed him, but he did not let them leave me. That means something, right?

In front of us, a lady is trying to get glass out her car so she can sit on the seat. She's got her sleeves around her hands, raking shards out. Blood starts to stain her baby-blue shirt. She's shaking. She looks kinda like the lady from the beauty supply store I go to. I look closer and—yup, that's her. She pretty cool, always helpful. She yells at her husband when he starts following me around the store like I'm gonna steal his damn nail polish. I want to help her, but I can't stop. Black's got ahold of me, and he ain't looking around like we at a carnival. He movin'.

Behind us, a bullhorn crackles, and then a loud voice is yelling at people to get off the street. I look over my shoulder and see the po po behind us too. They got more men up at the top of Seventh, got us barricaded in on both sides. They funneling us up the street toward the wagons they surely got waiting somewhere.

The crowd gets more hyped up and starts closing in on us, trying to get themselves up against the buildings like we are. One guy barrels right at Campbell. Black reaches around me and tries to grab her by the arm, but she pulls away and jumps aside. The man crashes past, but she got out of his way in time.

"My bad," Black says. He sounds shocked, and he lookin' at her like he can't believe she moves that fast.

Yeah, bet he didn't expect that, but he has no idea what we been through. We been almost killed a trillion times. We wide-awake and on full alert, and that's how we've made it through the night.

Then this black dude wearing a fly-ass green slouch beanie and a RESIST shirt jumps out of the crowd and stands in front of us. Campbell actually bumps into this one. "You Lena?" he yells at me.

I'm so shocked, I nod before I think about why I'm telling some stranger who I am.

Beanie man yells again, waving over my head at someone. "I got 'em! I found your cousin and the white girl."

Cousin? I spin around—and oh snap! Marcus! He's shoving his way through the crowd toward me. My cousin grabs hands with Beanie Man and daps him up. "Thanks, Rahim."

As Rahim takes off, Marcus grabs me in a hug, which is awkward because Black's still gripping my arm, so I don't get away from him. I'm crying all over again.

"Lena! Man, I'm glad I found you," Marcus says.

Black tugs on my arm, and I let go of my cousin. Black pulls me in closer.

"She's good, bruh," Black says. "I got her."

I'm loving this protective version of Black, but he might want to back down when Marcus is concerned. My cousin only went to jail because he got caught with a little weed in his car, but don't think because you see him preaching around the neighborhood, he won't whoop your ass, because he will.

"Oh, you got her, do you?" Marcus barks. "Where was you when this became a situation?"

Black shrugs. "Seems to me like you ain't have her then neither, 'cuz when she found me, she was alone."

"I ain't gotta explain myself to you," Marcus says. He puts a hand on Campbell's shoulder. "Lena, I got your little friend. Let's go."

"I'm going with Black," I say.

Campbell elbows me. "What? No, we should go with your cousin."

"You should listen to your girl." Marcus pats Campbell's shoulder like he's proud of her. "She seem to have more sense than you at the moment. Pops would want you with me."

Of course, Black responds to that. "Dude, you trippin'. She said she ain't going with you, so back up."

"Trust me when I tell you, this ain't what you want, playa," Marcus says.

"Try me."

Marcus pushes Black, and he falls over a bench onto his ass.

I scream. "What the hell, Marcus?"

Black jumps up quick, but his lips curl. He turns, and I see a tear in his pants. He reaches back to feel the flapping pocket fabric and then he charges Marcus like a bull, head-first into Marcus's belly. They both hit the ground. These fools are rolling around on top of each other in the middle of the street, even though people are stampeding like a game of Jumanji started. I run over to split them apart, and Marcus accidentally punches me in the arm.

"Ouch!" I back up a step and rub my arm.

Black untangles himself from Marcus and stands. "You hit her, you loser!"

"Lena, cuz, I am so sorry," Marcus says. "I would never hit you on purpose."

"I know, we good," I say. But one look at Black's face, and I'm clear we are not good.

"They're coming with me," Black says.

I look over at Campbell's face, and she's terrified. All this time, we were running from wild situations, and now, she in another one, thanks to the crazy men in my life. I have to put a stop to this.

"Marcus, I'm going with Black. That's the end."

He stares at me. "I can't believe you. You gon' side with him after he put his hands on me?"

"Don't make it about that, Marcus. There are no sides. We have to move as a unit until this is over."

"You know what? I'm done participating in this fiasco. You wanna be up under this bum, that's on you." Marcus spins around and starts walking away. "I'm out."

25

CAMPBELL

Seventh Avenue

Oh no. No, no, no, no, no. He's going. Marcus is walking away. He just found us, and he's already leaving?

"Wait." The word emerges as a whisper, which fades away in all the noise around us.

I can't believe Lena's worthless boyfriend started this shouting match. Like there's not enough to worry about already? He wants to fight too? That is so not normal.

I want to run, but can't think where to go. The police have started thinning the crowd—throwing people to the ground and slapping zip ties on them. My jaw clenches as I scan a row of black guys sitting on the sidewalk, hands cuffed behind their back. All of them wear those protest shirts. What the hell? Who cares about their signs and the fact that they're blocking the road? What about the guys who looted my dad's store? What about the people on a stealing spree? They should find those people and arrest them.

Cops power through the crowd. When I've seen footage of a riot on TV, once the police arrive, it seems like they restore calm. I want so badly to see the riot squad marching down Seventh as a good sign. A sign all this is going to be over soon. But my knees won't stop shaking. *Soon* might not be soon enough for us. We're still in the middle of this story, and the ending doesn't feel close. This is an explosion that goes on and on and on. In reality, no one on this street is safe, no matter what they're doing out here.

No matter if they're just like us—trapped where they don't want to be.

An inferno rages on Seventh Avenue to the north of us. That patio, more cars, the tire place. I can't tell at this point what all's burning. I feel like everything is.

"We have to go," I say to no one. Because no one is listening to me.

Marcus steps off the curb into the street, shouting and gesturing wildly. Black follows him, hand stretched out to shove. Lena snatches the back of his shirt.

"Nah, baby," she yells. "Let him go."

Black strains against her hold, his shirt plastered against him. "If your cousin wasn't holdin' me back, I'd be on you."

Marcus slides back a step, taunting Black, smirking at him. "You gon' let your shawty control you?"

"You lucky she here!" He slaps his chest with his palm, all puffed up—but honestly he doesn't seem to be pulling away from Lena. He's probably a foot taller than she is. If he really pulled, he'd break her hold in a second.

The fight looks like a horribly choreographed scene in a school play. Like Lena realizes she doesn't need to really hold him because Black isn't really going to go after Marcus. And Marcus clearly feels the same because he doesn't have his fists up to defend himself. The whole episode pisses me off. I want to yell at them to stop being so awful, but then I notice three cops behind Marcus in the street. Fire reflects off their plastic masks. One holds a baton over his head.

"Look out!" I shriek.

Lena jolts. "Black!"

She yanks him back. Lena James has a surprising amount of strength. Black is five steps back in a second. Marcus isn't so lucky. He pivots, trying to see what's coming at him, but in that same moment, a rioter lunges into the street beside him, heaving a bent-up metal bike frame over Marcus's head—right at the cops. They jump and scatter but one's not quick enough. The bike smashes into his shins, felling him. Another goes after the rioter. The third cop comes at us. Marcus gets caught in melee. A baton crashes down on his shoulder, bringing him to his knees. Through the black-clad legs of the officers, I see his mouth open in a scream, his arms go up, swinging wildly. The baton comes down again. And again. Marcus's body falls forward, his forehead cracks against the asphalt, so loud I can hear it over all the other noise.

"No," Lena wails. She jumps toward him, but Black grabs her from behind, locking his arms around her waist. She fights against his hold. "Not my cousin!"

"Let's go," yells Black. "He'd want you to get somewhere safe."

"But he's hurt. We can't leave him."

"He'll be okay. They'll take him to the hospital," I say, hoping that's true more than knowing it. "They have to."

"Yeah, they will," Black says. "But we gotta get out of here or we'll be next."

The words are as sharp as the starter pistol at a track meet. My body coils, tensed and frozen for a second, then I'm running. My feet pound to the rhythm of the words that circle around in my mind: *Get out, get out.* I want to see what's happening to Marcus, but I can only focus on Black, who's in front of me, pushing Lena along. She's sobbing, but she doesn't pull away. She lets him shove her forward, though she keeps looking back.

"Where are we going?" I shout. "We can't just run!"

"My car down at the Walmart," Black replies.

Suddenly, I'm bursting with energy. We have a destination. Finally. Walmart. It's only a few blocks to the south, at the end of the commercial district. If we can get there, there will be a car. And we will get home. I lift my knees, sprint flat out, passing Lena and Black.

"Damn!" Black pants. "Lena, your girl some kinda Usain Bolt."

I don't stop. I dodge, sliding around people and cops and debris, until I hit the block before the Walmart. Until I see the parking lot.

I slam on the brakes. "Oh, hell."

They catch up quickly. I'm doubled over when they do, trying to get my breath back, but I can tell when they see it too. When they realize how colossally screwed we are.

"Damn!"

A helicopter hovers overhead with a spotlight sweeping over a mass of cop cars. SWAT vans. Command tents. Gear. All things Black is not going to want to run toward. *Can't* run toward. We're never going to be able saunter into that parking lot, say: *Excuse me, officers, if we could get in that car and be on our way.* Maybe I could do that. This black guy I'm with, though? Lena? No way.

"My car," Black moans.

"Come on!" Lena shrieks. She whirls around and starts moving back up the street. "Can't stand here! Can't stay here!"

I'm with her. This is a dead end—but where to instead?

We start back the way we came, but there's no way out

up there. Nobody's thinking. Nobody's got a plan. We get two blocks up the street before a car screeches to a halt beside us.

"Peanut!" Black shouts, leaping toward the car.

The sedan is blue and vaguely familiar, but I can't think why. I can't think at all. Black's crew is in the car already. Black jumps into the front seat and pulls Lena onto his lap. Someone opens the back door for me. I duck and get caught. I struggle and strain, but I'm stuck. I can't move! I can't—

Hands yank my backpack from my shoulders. "Hey!" I try to turn, reaching for my disappearing bag.

"Move, white girl, move!"

"Get in!"

People are shouting at me, and I'm half in and half out of the car door, wedged. My backpack's gone, taken by one of the guys by the back of the car. The trunk opens. I give up worrying about that, join the scramble to pack in more bodies than can fit into the little sedan. Behind me, the trunk slams shut. Someone jumps into the driver's seat. Another guy, overweight and dressed in too-baggy clothes, wearing a bright white ball cap, shoves his way into the car next to me, and we take off with a squeal of tires, fishtailing wildly.

The crowd in the car stifles me. As does the smell. Of the seven people sardined in here, five are sweaty, smelly guys. Not even the air freshener labeled NEW CAR SMELL dangling from the rearview mirror overcomes the stench. I try to breathe through my mouth, but I only end up tasting the sourness of the sweat. My stomach rolls.

I sit sideways, half holding up my own weight on the console between the front seats and half sitting on this guy's knee. My arms shake with the effort of keeping my butt off a stranger's thigh. We take a sharp right and hit a pothole on one of the roads heading toward Grant Village. The car bounces, and my head slams against the ceiling.

"Whoa, Grand Theft Auto!" yells one of the guys in the back with me. "Take it easy there, killa!"

Everyone else laughs. Like they're not scared anymore. Like this is all some big adventure.

I have never hated any moment more than this one. I glare at Lena, and then my stomach sinks. She's buried her face in Black's neck, and she's silent, but the slight heaving of her shoulders gives her away. She's crying, and I think I can guess why. Poor Marcus. I want to reach through the seats and touch her shoulder, comfort her. A wave of nausea rolls through me when I think of the sound his head made hitting the pavement. We shouldn't have left him. I shouldn't have told her he was okay—I couldn't know that. That moment was wild, the noise, the smoke, the police, that bicycle flying straight for them. What could we have done? Getting away seemed like the smartest—the only—thing to do. But we left him. The blood drains from my head, leaving me dizzy. We left Marcus.

I watch helplessly as Lena cries, blinking fast to prevent my own waterfall, muzzled by my own confusion. There are no words to say.

The car never slows as we blaze through the streets of Grant Village. We streak past a crowd of people running from the riot, other cars that managed to get away, like us, speeding carelessly down the road. All that traffic thins to a trickle within a few streets. As crazy as Seventh was, just a few blocks over, and we're already safe. It doesn't seem real.

"Did you see how I took out that one Five-O with the stick, man?"

"What you talkin' 'bout, Big Baby? You was too busy runnin' to take out anyone."

"Yeah, Big Baby. Old po po probably trip on his boots."

"Nah, cuz, you just didn't see."

My stomach clenches. How can they laugh? How can they remember exactly what happened? The entire night blurs in my mind like a toddler's finger painting. Every memory I have since the *pop pop pop* of the gunshots at the football field is all shape and color with no form.

The guys go on laughing and blustering about what they did and didn't do during the riot. Lena's holding on to Black's arm, rhythmically zipping the zipper on the sleeve of Black's jacket. Soothing herself until her sobs slow, then stop.

I'm still too rattled to calm down. My muscles won't unclench, and my jaw hurts. Which means I've been grinding my teeth.

"Where you stay at, Campbell?" Lena asks softly.

I blink. "What?"

"Your house. Where we takin' you?"

"Takin' her?" Peanut demands. "What you mean, we takin' her to her house?"

"Don't be basic, Peanut." Lena puts a hand on her hip. "After all we went through, you gonna put a girl out on the street?"

"Chill out, red bone," Peanut says, his hands gripping the steering wheel. "She ain't my problem." He shoots a look right past Lena to Black that clearly says, *Control your woman*.

My nose wrinkles. I don't get why she puts up with these guys.

"I don't care," I say. The words come out slowly, a little runny at the edges. "Let me out. I can get home from here."

"Campbell," Lena says.

But she doesn't go on. What's she going to say—that I wouldn't be safe?

To my surprise, Black speaks up. "Take her to her place, Peanut." He slides the command reluctantly from the side of his mouth.

When Peanut doesn't object, I say, "Taylor Street. Just past Central."

Silence replaces the noise and laughter from a few minutes before, broken only by the rumbles of all of us breathing and waiting to see what's going to happen. Finally, Peanut nods. "Her place, then yo shawty place, then we done. Got me, Black?"

"Gotchu."

The drive takes another few minutes, and then we're pulling up to the curb of my father's dumpy little two-bedroom house. One of his neighbors has installed super-sensitive floodlights, which flash on as soon as we pull up.

Everyone flinches.

"Damn, yo. What's this all about?"

I don't bother to reply as I reach for the door handle. Which is hidden on the other side of a mile of flabby stomach.

"Let me out," I say.

"Aw, come on, white girl, you don't wanna hang around with us no more? Big Baby big all over. He real fun," teases the guy whose knee I'm on.

My face goes hot, and I clench my jaw, trying desperately not to react.

Lena's voice rings from the front seat. "Big Baby! Move yo behind out the way and let her out the car."

Big Baby does as she says, grumbling. I mutter *thanks* in Lena's direction and scramble out. Peanut's already revving the engine, about to take off. I'm glad to be rid of him—all of them—but I want my backpack. Only because Big Baby lumbers slowly back into the car do I have a second to grab the door handle.

"I need my things." The words dribble out in a whisper, and I have to try again. "I want my backpack."

The engine roars, and for a second, in which my heart pounds painfully, I think Peanut's going to ignore me and drive off. But then, Black says, "Pop the trunk, Peanut."

"It's broke," he says. "Don't open from here. Never mind, man."

I grab the handle like I'm going to be able to keep the car there by holding on. "No! I want my bag!" I must sound so silly, but I don't care.

"Lena'll bring it to you tomorrow."

"Get my name out yo mouth, Peanut. You don't speak for me," she says.

"Yo, get the girl her gear, man," someone says from the back seat. "We gotta leave."

With an angry growl, Peanut jumps out of the car and walks around to the back. Over the roof, he points the keys at me, and says, "Stay there."

He seems more tense than he did walking down Seventh. I shake my head. Guess the adrenaline is wearing off for everyone. I lean into Lena's window. "Hey. Thanks."

She nods. I pause. I don't know what I'm waiting for. But I guess that's all we have for each other. No hug. No big buddy moment. This is all. With a shrug, I make my way to the back of the car.

"Told you to stay there!" Peanut shouts as he pops the trunk.

God, he's uptight. "I just want my backpack."

I duck under his outstretched arm. He grabs the back of my shirt and jerks me away, but not before I catch sight of the contents of the trunk. My mouth goes dry. Boxes of drills. A wet/dry vacuum. A stack of hammers. A handsaw. Blue-and-white boxes of energy-saver light bulbs. Never-opened boxes, tools with price stickers—all brand new. All merchandise you'd find in a hardware store. In my *father's* hardware store. I flash back on one vivid memory from the chaos of the night—a light blue sedan parked in my father's usual space in the alley beside the store. I look from the looted goods to my backpack, dangling from Peanut's outstretched arm, to his furious face, and rage floods through me.

"That's our stuff!" I scream, rushing him. "You stole it!"

26

LENA

Campbell's House

Campbell yells, and Big Baby jumps out the car. I lean out the window to see what's going on, and Campbell's jumping at Peanut, and Big Baby holding her back. What is happening? Campbell's been a lot of things tonight, but drama for no reason? That she ain't been. If she's mad, there's a reason.

"Sounds like shawty givin' him the business," Wink says.

"Let's see what's up," I say to Black. He's not looking like he's trying to move, but I ain't gonna leave her out there like this. "Black, move!"

I get out and walk toward Campbell. "What's going on?"

She flips her hand in the direction of the car. "Just look."

I see the tools in the trunk. I'm not *for sure*-for sure, but I swear, this looks like what you'd get at a hardware store.

"Peanut," I say. "This better not have came from where I think it did."

"Oh, you a detective now, Lena?" He throws his hands in the air in frustration.

Black walks up behind me, and his mouth drops open. "Damn!"

If you put two and two together, these tools came from Campbell's dad store, and that's why she goin' off. I don't blame her either. She was messed up over seeing all that destruction, and to think she done rode in the car with the person that robbed her daddy's spot. I can't stop staring into the trunk, all that brand-new hardware junk. Gotta be worth a whole lot of cash, if Peanut bothered to steal it. Yeah, Campbell better than me because I might have busted him in the head if he jacked my pops.

"Damn, Peanut," Black says again. He never repeats himself like this. His hand finds the front of his shirt and crumples it up, which he only does when his spirit is hurting. "This what you was up to when you disappeared on us before?"

"I don't owe no explanation to you or this bitch!"

"Aw, hell nah." I suck in a breath. "How you callin' her a bitch, and you stole from her?"

"The whole damn town was stealin'."

I shake my head. "A thief believes everybody steals."

"Here comes Saint Lena again." Peanut rolls his eyes.

"Bruh," Black says in a warning tone.

Peanut focuses on Campbell, who's eyeing the tools in the trunk real hard. "Don't even think about it."

Her face turns red. "All of this is from my dad's store! You better give it back."

"White girl heated, ain't she?" Big Baby whispers. He shifts the brim of his cap around uncomfortably. That ain't no surprise. Big Baby kinda soft.

"You would be too if somebody got you for yo' stuff," I snap. "Peanut, I know for a fact you cracked a fool upside the head for jacking you. But you acting all shocked Campbell's mad? That ain't right."

"Bump this. I'm out," Peanut says.

"Black," I say.

He sighs like he can't believe what he's about to say next. "I can't let you pull off, homie."

"What?" Peanut side-eyes Black.

Black turns to Big Baby for backup, but he holds up his hands. "I didn't know this stuff belonged to my future baby mama."

Oh, lord. Big Baby too?

His joke don't go over with Campbell at all. She look like she got hit in the face by a door. "No way!" she cries.

He's trying to lighten the moment, but this boy never was good at knowing what would make a girl mad. "Nothing's funny, Big Baby."

217

"So y'all all did this?" Black shakes his head. "We make music. When did y'all become thieves?"

"What difference do it make, my dude?" Wink says, stepping out of the car. "Ain't *yo* stuff."

"This is whack, and it ain't what we do. Ain't suppose to be what we do."

While Black is arguing with them, I reach into the trunk, grab an armload, and march onto Campbell's porch. After I drop the first round, Campbell gets the hint and starts helping. A few times, I attempt a smile at her, but she don't smile back. I understand, she hot. I hope she don't think I would have put her in the car with these thieves if I knew they robbed her daddy. I wouldn't have put *myself* in this position. I'm not like those girls who're all ride or die, willing to catch a case for love.

"What are y'all doing?" Peanut yells when he catches sight of us. He starts toward Campbell, but she throws a heavy gizmo at him. She misses, but Peanut has to duck and stop.

"Stay back! This all belongs to my family!"

I'm kinda diggin' turnt Campbell. She right. It's hers. We ain't gotta feel no type of way about taking it back. Me and this girl been through hell tonight. This punk ain't gon' scare us. What they gon' do, jump us? No. So Imma keep moving boxes 'til they're all on the porch.

"Peanut, just let the girls get that shit out the trunk," Black says.

Peanut comes back around toward Campbell for a second time, revving up like a race car. My stomach tightens. Every time I seen him do that before, somebody got hit. He heads to the porch—following Campbell. Black moves too, snatching up a hammer. "I would hate to crack you in the head, bruh, but I will."

I sneak a glance at Campbell as she reaches the porch. She been pretty stone-faced since I got out the car, but she breaks a little at that, like she's as surprised as me and Peanut to hear Black talking like this. To be honest, I'm kinda proud too. Black don't back down, even when Peanut challenges him.

"Over some dumb-ass white girl?"

"This ain't about her. It's about you riskin' the music, everything we workin' for, our legacy, for a couple a bucks and some power tools."

Peanut starts shouting. "Oh, you wanna talk about how we fund the music? Where you think we get the stacks to spend a week in the studio? You think working yo' Best Buy minimum-wage job gonna get us more than a minute in there, fool? It ain't! You worry 'bout the beats. I worry about the cash flow."

"This don't make you a baller. You're gonna wind up a guest of the state," Black says, gesturing with the hand holding the hammer. He's so mad, spit's flying out as he talks. "Ain't no recording studios in jail."

"You already been takin' that risk whether you knew it or not," he says. "You're guilty by association." He lifts a foot like he gonna get closer.

I see a couple people walking this way. They look a little torn up, like they just came from where we did. Maybe once Peanut realizes he has an audience, he'll shut this down. But he ain't that smart.

"Another step," Black warns. "And Imma rock yo' skull."

"Oh, yeah? That gonna be before or after I put a bullet in yours?" Peanut lifts the corner of his undershirt and pulls out a gun.

I scream and jump toward Black, but Campbell grabs me. She's screaming too. Those people I saw coming up the street, they scatter.

"Don't, don't, don't," Campbell begs. "You'll get shot!"

"Stay back, baby." Black's voice trembles. I never heard him sound that way and that freaks me out so bad because I don't know what any of 'em could do next. They friends; they don't never treat each other this way.

I scan the windows of all the houses I can see, hoping people looking. This can't go like this. But even if somebody did call 911, nobody coming. The police are all down at Seventh.

Campbell tucks her arm into mine and squeezes. She pulls back harder. "Lena, please. Come on!"

I fade back, but Peanut hollers, waving the heat.

"Everybody be still! Next person that moves is gettin' popped."

Me and Campbell freeze. He sounds wild. All the boys are talking over top of each other too. They sound scared.

"Peanut, man, you trippin'," Big Baby says. "Put the gun down."

"You gon' shoot me, Peanut?" Black asks. "That's how this night gon' end?"

"No!" I'm crying. Bawling, really. I can't get more words out. Please, God, don't let this be happening.

"Shut up, Lena," Peanut says.

Black steps up to block Peanut from mean-mugging me.

"Milton Samuels," Wink says, speaking for the first time in a while. Him using Black's government name makes me stop breathing. "You don't wanna get no closer, Milton."

"Please don't," I whisper. "Please."

"See, Milton? You got your girl all in tears. You let us walk away with this lick, and she can stop cryin'."

"You're not going anywhere with our crap!" Campbell shouts.

Big Baby grunts and slices his hand across his throat, his eyes real wide. "Girl, be quiet, you tryna die?"

Black spreads his hand out. "No one gotta die tonight."

"Nobody know that yet," Peanut says.

Over a buncha hammers and nails? It doesn't have to go this way. Campbell's got every right in the world to take

221

all this back. Yet my man got some fire at his head? My heart about to pound right out of my chest. Everybody's frozen. Suddenly, the street goes dark. That neighbor's lights go off.

"What happened?"

There's more yells, and Black hollers. I can make out the shape of him going flying toward where Peanut was standing.

"Black, don't!" I scream.

A gunshot. Me and Campbell drop to the ground. The security lights flash back on. I peek up, and Black and Peanut are wrestling. Black goes for the steel. Peanut sticks him in the jaw, but Black is still able to knock the pistol away. It slides across the grass. Big Baby leans over, trying to separate the boys. He ends up with an elbow hooked around Peanut's neck. Wink jumps in, grabbing Big Baby's bicep. Black starts to slide loose and go after the gun.

"Wink," Big Baby yells. "Stop."

He lets go of Peanut, reaches out an arm, and pushes Wink so hard he goes down. Big Baby don't go back after Black and Peanut. Instead, he lunges for the banger.

"That's enough!" he yells, snatching up the piece. He cryin'. Hell, we *all* cryin'. "We done."

They listen to him, like they always do when it really matter. Thank God. Black and Peanut ease off each other and stand up. Everybody breathing hard.

Black wipes some blood off his mouth and says, "Lena, get whatever is left out the trunk."

Big Baby releases the clip and lowers the steel to hang by his side. Campbell and I scramble to put the last boxes on the porch. There's not much left, and we get done quickly once Black starts helping us. Peanut so mad he can't talk, but he don't press up on us no more. Wink's on the ground, groaning. He rolls over onto his knees and struggles to his feet. As Campbell and I wait on the steps, Black walks to the end of the sidewalk, to Big Baby. They stare at each other.

"We brothers," Black says. "This ain't how we do each other."

"Black," Big Baby pleads.

He shakes his head.

Wink hauls himself into the passenger seat, still kinda in pain from going down. Peanut looks at Big Baby. "Where you stand?"

Big Baby looks at Black again, his big, sweet face all wet from crying. Then he moves toward the car.

"Don't do it, man," Black says.

"C'mon, Big Baby," I say. "You don't have to go with them."

"Yeah, I do," he says, shaking his head. He wipes his face with his collar, scrubbing off all the tears and sweat and leaving a stain on his T-shirt. "Somebody gotta talk to them."

He follows Peanut into the car, and they drive off. Black stands there, watching them go like he a statue.

Campbell's back up on her porch, messing with her keys.

"Campbell," I say.

"Go away, Lena."

The porch is dark since those security lights don't really reach here. I get close to try to see her face. She hides it from me.

"We can help you bring this in," I whisper.

"No."

PART V

AFTER MATH

27

CAMPBELL

Campbell's House

The screech of tires in the street signals Peanut's exit, with the rest of his gang. They're gone. I'm home, but somehow I don't feel the relief I expected.

I'm so numb, I can barely process where I'm standing. Outside my house. On the porch. The weathered floor-boards beneath my feet are familiar, as is the milk crate full of my dad's old newspapers beside the door. And all around that, the remains of his store, the scraps of merchandise we salvaged from Peanut's car. The getaway car of the thieves who robbed him. The getaway car I just rode home in.

That is *so* messed up. Not more messed up than a fight over a gun in my front yard, though.

God, this night.

"Campbell Soup, let us help you move these packages inside, okay?"

I glance over my shoulder. Lena clutches an armload of tools against her stomach. Black stands behind her with a look I can't quite figure out. Mad and scared and maybe a little sheepish. Like he's embarrassed by his friends.

Well, he should be. The sight of the store's inventory in their hands sends me into a rage again.

"My dad didn't have anything to do with all this!" I shout. "He worked so hard, and that place was all he had! He had nothing to do with the governor or the police or the fight at school or any of it. That place, his store—it's just there."

"People be mad, Campbell," Lena says. "They gotta express that somehow. They ain't thinkin'. You gotta understand—"

"I don't," I hurl back. "I'll never understand why people think stealing is the answer. And I can't believe you're defending looters!"

She drops the tools she's carrying, then clutches her head, like she's about to tear her hair out. "I'm sorry about what happened to your store. But you were there. It didn't start out about looting or all that. Did them news people show up before, when they was having a peaceful protest? Was anybody listening when they tried to approach things in a civil manner? No. But when shops start burning down, here they come. I'm not defending looters, but you're not even trying to understand. When you push people to their breaking point, and they ain't got no power, they'll find a way to take it. What's so wrong with that?"

I've got no answer. Because I don't know what's wrong and what's right. I don't get this neighborhood or how people here feel. I don't understand Black's friends stealing or pulling guns on each other. I don't get those white guys with their Confederate flags antagonizing everyone. Me and my dad, we're both caught up in circumstances neither of us understand—something about wrong place, wrong time comes to mind. My father has lived here for twenty years, and I realize I've never seen him be friendly with his neighbors or his customers or other shop owners on Seventh, except the Wellses, and he doesn't invite them to hang out at his house or anything. Maybe he wouldn't be so surprised to find people think of him as an outsider. I don't know how he feels. It never occurred to me to ask.

Lena's right—I haven't *tried* to understand this place at all.

The shout that had been winding up inside me dies. There's no one here to yell at but Lena and Black, and I'm not mad at them. Underneath my fury, I get that them standing up for me is a big deal. They could have let Peanut rob us. They owe me nothing, but they still helped. They're still here with me, not driving away with their friends.

I don't know what I would have done if our roles were reversed.

I only know I've never wanted to be alone so much in my life. For once, somebody stuck around, and I can't enjoy it. My body is coiled tight enough to snap, trying to keep me on my feet, and I don't think I'll be able to relax until I can close myself inside my dad's house, lie on the couch in the dark, and cry. I need Lena and Black to go home.

"Forget it," I say. I reach for the tools at Lena's feet. She bends, arms outstretched, wanting to help, but I jerk away the boxes before she can touch them. My eyes rise to meet hers. She blinks and backs off. I start dragging boxes into our living room. Lena hesitates on my porch for another second, watching me. Black shakes his head, grabs her hand, and heads down the steps into the yard, pulling her after him.

I'm sticking my foot in the screen door to hold it open so I can maneuver the jackhammer through, when the squealing of car tires makes me jump. The door thwacks closed, and the heavy tool falls from my hands. A car bumps over the curb and screeches to a stop on our grass. My father jumps out, not bothering to shut the door behind him. He races across the lawn, flinging himself toward Lena and Black.

"Get outta here, you punks!"

Black pushes Lena behind him and starts yelling back. "Dude, back up! Tonight ain't the night."

I'm trembling. How much more drama before we're finally safe? My father digs his phone from his pocket, and I register the words *calling the cops*.

Oh, God. No. Whatever he's thinking, no. No cops. No more trouble.

"Dad, don't," I call.

"Get inside, Campbell."

For the space of one breath, I consider turning my back and doing as he says. How do I even begin to explain all that's happened tonight? I can't. I imagine curling into a ball, closing my eyes, and leaving this for someone else to deal with. I can't do that either. This isn't Lena's fault—or Black's. None of tonight is their fault. And I've had my eyes closed long enough.

I jump down the steps and take the phone from my dad's hands.

"Campbell, I said go inside," my dad spits. He's more agitated than I've ever seen.

"No. They're my friends. Leave them alone."

"What? But Nicky called. He told me you were at his grandparents' place. And these things"—he glances around the porch at the remnants of his store—"he said they were looting! These people—"

"Not them, Dad."

He shakes his head. "I don't understand. How did all this end up here? What happened to dinner after the football game and your teacher?"

My stomach drops. I start spitting out words, not sure they make sense, but filling the air so he can't interrupt. "A bunch of people started fighting during the game, and it got out of control. We couldn't stay there, and Ms. Marino couldn't get to me, so Lena and I went down to Seventh, because Black—"

My father frowns. Man, I should have used his real name! Milton sounds so much less threatening.

"I mean, Milton has a car. But Seventh…" I shake my head. "When we saw what happened to the store, we saved what we could. Without their help, we wouldn't even have this."

Lena's mouth falls open. She catches my gaze, and I shrug. She didn't expect me to lie. I didn't expect to either. But my dad calling the cops on Lena and Black would be one more wrong in the longest night of wrongs in my entire life.

For once, she doesn't know what to say. That's probably for the best. Whatever she says will just draw my dad's attention to her.

"I'm—I'm—" He blinks fast, like he's holding back tears. I cringe because I have never seen my father cry. "The store?"

A tear drips down my nose. "It's bad, Dad."

"I should be down there, standing guard."

"No! Seventh is not safe. And there's nothing left to save."

"Nothing?" he whispers. When I don't respond, he heaves a shaky breath and staggers toward the front steps, flopping down with his head in his hands, repeating, "Nothing. Nothing."

The three of us, Black and Lena and me, watch my father break down.

I lean toward Lena and whisper, "You should go."

Before my father recovers and starts the interrogation. Questions like, where's that car Black supposedly drove us home in, for starters. Lena hesitates, but Black doesn't. He grabs her hand and pulls her toward the street. She resists for a second, looking back at me.

"Campbell," she says.

I know the words that are getting stuck in her throat. They're the same ones that won't come out of mine.

So I nod. "Text me you got home okay."

She nods back.

I sit on the steps besides my father, watching as Black and Lena disappear into the night. My dad is not much of a hugger, but to my surprise, he slides an arm around my shoulders and tucks me to his side.

"I'm sorry about the shop, Dad."

"I'm sorry I wasn't here tonight."

I thought my tears had run completely dry, but more swell in my eyes. I wipe them away with my knuckle. "It's okay."

"We have a lot to talk about," he says. "But not tonight."

I nod. The night is still too chaotic for the questions he wants to ask, and I'm not ready to form the answers in my own mind. Maybe by morning I will be. For the moment, we sit in silence as hours pass, and the helicopters hovering in the sky dwindle to a few, and then none. The sirens fade into the distance. Smoke from the last-burning fires over on Seventh still drifts through the air as the sun rises. Not until the sky is fully light and the nighttime chill has burned off does my father finally seem ready to climb off the porch. A million phone calls await him, to his landlord and insurance brokers and my mom, as does a visit to the shop that will shatter him as thoroughly as the display window was shattered. He moves slowly, maybe trying to ward off reality for a few more minutes. Or maybe he's as tired and broken as I am.

As I stand to follow him back inside, my phone chimes with a text message from an unknown number—two words I know must be from Lena.

28

LENA

Lena's House

As we walk toward my home, neither me or Black talk.
With all the adrenaline gone, pain shoots through me. My
feet are swollen, and every strap of my remaining sandal
feels like a razor blade. I stop to take the shoes off. One is so
busted, and they're both dirty and scratched. These sandals
are tired and through. I dump them in the first trash can
I see, adding to the long list of tragic events of the night.
Now, I'm barefoot, trying to lift my feet in a way that they
don't hit the pavement so hard, but that's not helping. I
probably look goofy. I don't care. I'm just trying to drag
across the finish line.

We're on my block. There are a few houses lit up along
the street, all the ones I expect, like Ms. Arnold who keeps
her porch light on for her son who gets off work late. And
Pops who never turns off that front light until he knows

I'm inside. That light coming through our picture window is a welcoming arm, pulling me home.

"Lena," Black says. "I didn't know they did that."

Is he looking for something to say? 'Cuz I was okay with the silence. I'm tired. Too tired to talk, to explain, to understand, to go off, to care, to think at all.

"I know that."

If he wants to talk, he can discuss how, when that scuffle went down at my school, he could have come and got me. Had he done that, so much of this night would be different. Because I had to try to get to him, Marcus got hemmed up, and he's already on probation. I've gotta figure out how I'm going to deal with that. Black wants to ask questions, he can ask me why I'm walking like a circus clown. Ask me why I'm bloody. Ask me what happened between the time we talked and the time he saw me, because I know I was looking rough when I got to him. So ask me why.

I stand in the moist grass of my front yard and take a deep breath, letting it out as the cool grass squishes under my feet, soothing the cuts and easing the throbbing. With that relief, the noise around me turns back on, and I hear the sounds I'm used to, like the dog next door that's always barking and nobody knows why.

Black steps in front of me. We've done this before. From where Pops sits in his chair in the front room, he won't see us. Black leans in to kiss me, but I turn my head and his lips land on my cheek. I'm not feeling him right now.

"What's good?" he says.

"I'm cool."

"Then why you actin' funky toward me?"

I want to vomit up all of my emotions, but with the state I'm in, I may say something I can't take back. I stare off into space, and Black pulls me in to his chest.

"Lena, I'm sorry, baby."

I gently pull myself away from him. "The number I was callin' you from, can you text it to me?"

"Yeah."

"Go ahead. I don't want you to get home and forget."

I wait for him to send the text, then head up our front steps as Black's footsteps crunch away. There's no point in turning my key quietly in the lock. Pops is waiting for me.

"Hey, Pops."

"Yeah, come on in here," Pops says. "Beverly called, she said Marcus—"

I don't think Pops was expecting me to look like death warmed over, because his frown quickly turns into concern. Whatever speech he had prepared has left him. He stands, rushes across the room to grab my shoulders and spin me around to get a one-eighty look at me.

"Lena, you got blood on your clothes. What on God's green earth happened to you tonight?"

"A big fight broke out at my school."

"You were in the fight?"

"No, no, no, no, no. I was around, but I got myself out of there quick."

"How did you end up with Marcus?" Pops asks.

"The streets was blocked off. I couldn't get straight here. I passed him along the way, and he came with me for a while."

"How did he end up at the hospital while you came back here? I need to know the full story, Lena, 'cuz right now full of malarkey is the best description of you."

"I'm telling you the truth, Pops." Only part of it, but Imma see what I can get away with. Not much.

"This might be the truth, but it ain't the whole story."

"You're right, Pops. Can I promise to tell you everything tomorrow? I'm so tired. May I please take a shower and lie down?"

"No. There will be no showering, no relaxing, no nothin' 'til I get some answers."

I wish I could tell Pops a story he would be proud of—that I was marching with Black Lives Matter, like he did with King, or that I was down there trying to keep Marcus out of trouble instead of the opposite. But I'm too beat to lie.

"After the fight at school, I walked with a friend to meet up with Black to give us a ride."

"I should have known that thug was involved."

"Lemme finish, Pops. Marcus saw us and came with us. We walked into a protest that turned into a riot. Marcus got slammed on the ground by the police, and that's how he ended up in the hospital. Black and his boys got me and my friend outta there and to her house. After that, Black walked me home. A lot went on. I don't think this blood is mine. Other than sore feet, I'm okay. I just want to lie down, Pops. Please."

He lets out a long sigh. "All right, we'll finish this up in the morning."

"'Night, Pops."

Pops grabs me by the shoulders and kisses my forehead, and he examines me one more time.

"I'm okay," I say. "I promise."

The throbbing returns to my feet, and I stop by the linen closet and get down the foot tub, then go to the bathroom. Pieces of the night come flying back into my head as I fill the tub with hot water. I reach under the sink for some Epsom salt, 'cuz you know Pops can always be trusted to have that on hand, and sprinkle extra salts in the tub. A little water splashes on the floor as I head to my room, probably from the wobble in my walk because I hurt.

I sit on the edge of the bed, put my feet in the tub, and melt. Nothing has ever felt so amazing, not even those fancy bath bombs I love so much. I plug my phone into the extra charger by my bed and fall back.

I close my eyes. I can't even believe this night started with me watching the Dolls body their routine during the game and me begging Black for his attention. A quadrillion risings and settings of the sun have passed since then. And I lived 'em with Campbell of all people. I definitely wouldn't have picked her, but we gave this night the business. We held each other down. I hate that Black's friends stole me and Campbell's high-five moment. We earned that.

A few moments later, my phone comes on and dings like twenty times. I sit up and notice all the missed voice mails, texts, social media alerts, but I don't open them. I go to Black's text, but only to get the number I need.

Home safe.

ACKNOWLEDGMENTS

When we sat down to write these acknowledgements, we were overcome and humbled to realize how full our writing village is. A book is an enormous labor of love, and we are profoundly appreciative of all the love we've been shown. In gratitude for that, we promise we will strive to put as much and more back into the world. To our enormous regret, we can't name every single person, or this would be longer than the book, but please know how grateful we are for everyone who supported this story and us along the way.

Special thanks in particular to:

Everyone who gave so generously their time, experience, and expertise to help us render the events that take place in *I'm Not Dying with You Tonight* plausibly, thoughtfully, and gently, including: law enforcement officers Captain Tait Sanborn and James Steffens (ret.) of the Pasco Sheriff's Office, firefighter Tamala Watkins, as well as real-life riot survivors Matt Melvin, Tory Russell, and Robin Seeherman.

Our beta readers, Kate Goodwin, Rachael Allen, Nic Stone, David Arnold, Ash Parsons, J. D. Myall, Robyn and Hannah Lucas, Lashunda Simpson, and Breanna McDaniel. Lena and Campbell's story is infinitely better for your thoughts.

Nicole Castroman, who introduced us to the best thing to ever happen to us, which brings us to…

Tracey Adams and the entire aLit team. Your fierce belief in and advocacy for this book is the reason we're seeing our publishing dream come true. We're so grateful and thrilled we get to go on this wild ride with you.

Sourcebooks and the amazing team there who helped hone this story into the book it has become and escort it onto bookshelves, including: Steve Geck, Sarah Kasman, Cassie Gutman, Beth Oleniczak, and Stefani Sloma.

Christa Desir: You took such care with the voices in this book, we couldn't have dreamed of a more thoughtful, careful, or kind copy editor. Grateful to have had your eyes on these pages.

Annette Pollert-Morgan, who was among the first to fall for and champion Lena and Campbell's story.

The coffee shops and pizza joints around East Atlanta that gamely let us use their counter tops and patio tables as our "office," but most especially Urban Pie and Joe's East ATL.

Little Shop of Stories and its incredible crew helmed by Diane Capriola and Dave Shallenberger: you're an indefatigable and invaluable supporter of the kidlit community, the best kids bookstore in the universe (no shade to any of the other awesome bookshops), and the place where we first met.

Our friends and family and the fabulous community of YA writers in Decatur and beyond, all of whom endlessly plot-talked and brain-picked and writing-retreated and chit-chatted and slang-educated us as we wound our way through this story, including: Vicky Alvear Shecter, Marie Marquardt (who gives the BEST hugs in YA literature), Lucille Rettino, Mayra Cuevas, Jenn Woodruff, Maryann Dabkowski, Mark Oshiro, Vania Stoyanova, Jessi Esparza, Laurel Snyder, Dede Nesbitt, Connie Morrison, Tamika Newhouse, the Not So YA Book Club, YATL, Judy Schachner, Gerron Rose, hair wizard Rebecca Hardin, Cory Mo, Lem Collins, T-Dawg DaDon, IRL Milton, the real Wink Woodall, Emily and Izzy, and Uber passengers Scott and Mike.

We'd also like to add the following thanks:

From Gilly:

To my mother and father, Susan and Mickey, who let me read every book I got my hands on, who presided over epic dinner table debates about topics far bigger than my teenage self was mature enough to engage in but who, nevertheless, listened and took my thoughts seriously, and who made sure I always knew how utterly and deeply they believed in me. Every ounce of confidence I have stems from your love and support. Thank you.

To my children, Noam, Nadav, and Shalev, who are my everything, who shared their time with me with the kids who live in my head, who cheered my writing journey with all their strength, and who bring more joy and love into my world than I ever could have dreamed. I strive with everything I do to make you proud and to let you know how utterly and deeply I believe in you.

To my sister, Stacey, cheerleader and confidant, who I know I can count on always. I'm so grateful we have each other. Thank you for being the best sister I could have asked for.

From Kim:

To my supportive siblings, Audra and Darin.

To my mom, Lula, who introduced me to a love of reading with frequent visits to the library and never said no to the purchase of a book.

To my biggest fan and cheerleader, Duprano Martin.

To my mentor, Wanda Shelley, who taught me the importance of nurturing the minds of teen girls.

To my best friends, Reasha, Alvin, and Ciara, who have an unyielding faith in me and have shown me what love looks like when it truly comes with no conditions.

Last but not least, to the people who make my heart beat, Drake Williams, Tobias Truvillion, The Superwoman Squad, Akilah Coleman, and Khalimah Gaston.

ABOUT THE AUTHORS

Kimberly Jones is the former manager of the bookstore Little Shop of Stories and currently works in the entertainment industry.

Gilly Segal spent her college years in Israel and served in the IDF. She is currently a lawyer for an advertising agency. Visit gillysegal.com.

FIREreads

ⓢ #getbooklit

Your hub for the hottest young adult books!

Visit us online and sign up for our
newsletter at FIREreads.com

 @sourcebooksfire

 sourcebooksfire

 firereads.tumblr.com